D1232805

Tara — a Tigress

# Tara – a Tigress

Arjan Singh
Edited by John Moorehead

QUARTET BOOKS
LONDON   MELBOURNE   NEW YORK

First published by Quartet Books Limited 1981
A member of the Namara Group
27 Goodge Street, London W1P 1FD

Copyright © Arjan Singh, 1981

ISBN 0 7043 2282 X

**British Library Cataloguing in Publication Data**
Singh, Arjan
Tara — a Tigress.
1. Tiger Haven Reserve
2. Tigers
I. Title    II. Moorehead, John
599.74'428   QL737. C2
ISBN 0-7043-2282-X

Printed in Great Britain

To Mrs Indira Gandhi

# Contents

Illustrations

*Black and White*
Spring 1977. Tara *(photo: Ashish Chandola)*
January 1977. Tara, Harriet and Eelie at play *(photos: Arjan Singh)*
Spring 1977. Tara *(photos: Ashish Chandola)*
Spring 1977. Babu Lal watches as Tara playfully trips up Arjan Singh *(photos: Ashish Chandola)*
April 1980. Tara, having now lived in the wild for three years, is observed eating a buffalo with her male companion Old Crooked Foot *(photos: Hashim Tyatji)*
Spring 1977. Tara, Arjan Singh and Babu Lal *(photo: Ashish Chandola)*

*Colour*
Tara, aged three months, with Arjan Singh at Twycross Zoo *(Dave Dawson, Survival Anglia Ltd)*
Tara, aged five months *(Dieter and Mary Plage, Survival Anglia Ltd)*
Leaving Twycross Zoo for Tiger Haven, 30 July 1976 *(Philip King, Survival Anglia Ltd)*
Tara being loaded on to the flight for Delhi *(Philip King, Survival Anglia Ltd)*
The last leg of the journey *(Dieter and Mary Plage)*
17 September 1976, arrival at Tiger Haven *(Dieter and Mary Plage)*
Tara being rowed across the Neora River *(Arjan Singh)*
Tara, aged one year *(Dieter and Mary Plage, Survival Anglia Ltd)*
A walk in the sal forest in Dudhwa National Park . . .*(Mike Price)*
. . .and on through the elephant grass *(Dieter and Mary Plage, Survival Anglia Ltd)*
Arjan Singh and Tara playing, closely watched by Eelie *(Dieter and Mary Plage, Survival Anglia Ltd)*
Eelie's turn for a game *(Arjan Singh)*
Harriet the leopardess and Tara *(Arjan Singh)*

*Publishers' Acknowledgement*

The Publishers would like to thank Sarah Giles for her invaluable assistance at every stage of the production of this book.

# Foreword

I have known Arjan Singh for many years and have always admired how much he has done for wildlife and the preservation of nature in his native land, not to mention his success in establishing close personal relationships with individual animals.

As I myself have been rearing tigers and leopards at Frankfurt Zoo for many years, conducting scientific experiments with tigers and building up an almost continuous thirty-year-long association with African leopards, Arjan Singh's experiences have fascinated me – in particular the concept of captive-born cats being hand-reared and subsequently reintroduced into the wild.

I know that many other people will be drawn to the subject and will find these experiences thoroughly absorbing. I therefore welcome the appearance of this book which is certain to give much pleasure to a wide public.

Dr Bernhard Grzimek

# Acknowledgements

I am deeply indebted to Mrs Indira Gandhi, who granted me permission to attempt a Tiger Reintroduction Project; without her moral support it would surely have foundered in the rapids of bureaucratic and political obstruction. Also to Dr Bernhard Grzimek, who funded the project out of his compassion for the future of wild animals wherever they may be, and who wrote the Foreword. I would like to express my thanks to Survival Anglia and their cameramen Dieter Plage, Mike Price and Ashish Chandola for allowing me to make use of their photographs, and to my sister-in-law Mira and to Nita Bhagat who so kindly typed my original manuscript. I am beholden to many kind friends in London who have aided me in various ways, especially to Arabella Amory who found me a publisher, John Moorehead who helped in the preparation of the final text and Sarah Giles. Finally, my gratitude is infinite to Tara and her tribe of tigers who assisted in her transition to a wild state, thus dumbfounding the prophets of doom waiting eagerly in the wings to hurl febrile thunderbolts at a worthy cause.

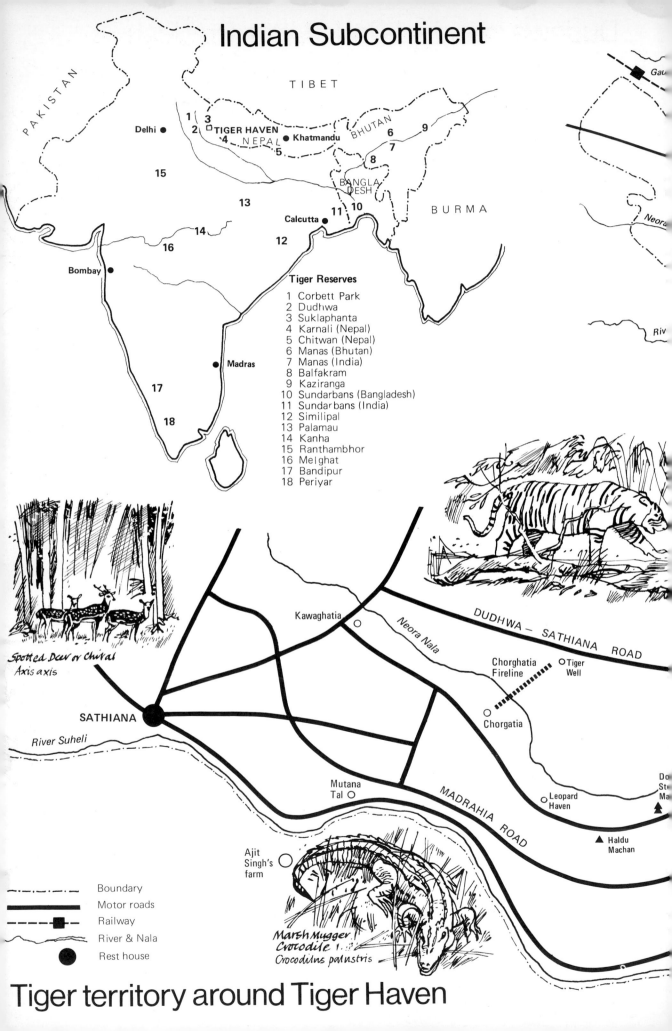

# Indian Subcontinent

TIBET

PAKISTAN

Delhi ●

1
3 □ TIGER HAVEN
2
4
NEPAL
5
● Khatmandu

BHUTAN

6
7
8

9

15

BANGLA DESH

BURMA

13

Calcutta ●

11 10

12

14

16

Bombay ●

● Madras

**Tiger Reserves**

1 Corbett Park
2 Dudhwa
3 Suklaphanta
4 Karnali (Nepal)
5 Chitwan (Nepal)
6 Manas (Bhutan)
7 Manas (India)
8 Balfakram
9 Kaziranga
10 Sundarbans (Bangladesh)
11 Sundarbans (India)
12 Similipal
13 Palamau
14 Kanha
15 Ranthambhor
16 Melghat
17 Bandipur
18 Periyar

17

18

Gau

Neora

Riv

Spotted Deer or Chital
Axis axis

Kawaghatia ○

Neora Nala

DUDHWA – SATHIANA ROAD

Chorghatia Fireline ○ Tiger Well

○ Chorgatia

SATHIANA

River Suheli

Mutana Tal ○

MADRAHIA ROAD

○ Leopard Haven

Do St Ma

▲ Haldu Machan

Ajit Singh's farm ○

Marsh Mugger Crocodile
Crocodilus palustris

Boundary
Motor roads
Railway
River & Nala
Rest house

# Tiger territory around Tiger Haven

# Dudhwa National Park : Uttar Pradesh

## NEPAL

River Mohana

BANKATI

MASANKHAMBH

CHANDANCHAUKI

BELAPARSUA

BELLRAIEN

CHHANGANALA

HIANA

DUDHWA

Tiger Haven

SONARIPUR

SALUKAPUR

QILA

River Suheli

## UTTAR PRADESH

---

GAURIPHANTA ROAD

ngris

TEAK TATION

DUDHWA

Am Chauraha

Prince's Monsoon Machan

Jungle Pool

Escarpment Machan

Tiger Copse

Am Danda Leopard Bridge

Jungle Fowl Jetty

Juliette Point

Kill Ford

Croc Pool

Croc Bend

TIGER HAVEN

Gran's Cage

Junction Bridge

Twin Lakes

Ghulli

River Suheli

Tiger Haven

Nakauhwa

Machan

Grey Langur
Presbytis entellus

Paul Sharp 3/81

kh

# Chapter 1

# Tara – A Tigress

The moon rose slowly above the giant silk-cotton tree, lending a soft phosphorescent lustre to its pink flowers. All day the soaring tree had been pulsating with orioles, drongos, mynahs, starlings, bulbuls and others who came to sip the nectar of the fleshy pods which would soon produce a kapok much in demand by the local inhabitants. Now it was almost devoid of birdlife apart from an Indian griffon vulture nesting in a crotch more than eighteen metres above the ground, where the thick perpendicular trunk coppiced into innumerable shoots. In the white radiance of the moonlight the vulture's elongated olive-green neck took on the eerie appearance of a hooded serpent. Further up the tree a number of peacocks had roosted for the night, and the echoes of their plaintive catcalls as they arrived had scarcely died away. Suddenly the stillness was shattered by a guttural roar. For a moment there was silence, followed by the falsetto alarm calls of chital grazing in a nearby glade and the protesting shrieks of the roosting peacocks. The two tigers which I knew as Old Crooked Foot and the Big Tigress were mating in the Tiger Copse, and the explosive sounds of their courtship would continue intermittently for another three days and nights, the two animals remaining there without food until the tigress conceived.

For over five years I had been engaged in an attempt to reintroduce domestically-reared leopards into the forest near my home at Tiger

1

Haven in northern India, and now it suddenly occurred to me that I might try the same experiment with a tiger. Admittedly, at least part of my enthusiasm derived from the romantic appeal of living with the world's master predator. After all, leopards had been virtually eliminated from the forests and there had been good reason for attempting to reintroduce them; by comparison the position of the tiger was fairly safe for the present, and the only valid reason was to demonstrate that such an animal could be taken from a zoo, hand-reared and then returned to the wild state. Such an experiment would not be easy. Indian national parks and sanctuaries did not provide the ideal conditions; they were too small and commercially orientated to maintain a viable genetic pool for a predator of such demanding dimensions as the tiger with its solitary nature, territorial requirements and need for large prey. (In Sri Lanka where the leopard with its smaller and more catholic feeding habits was the major predator, the parks were more secure and up to 1,295 square kilometres in area.) Moreover, in India the human population was expanding at the phenomenal rate of four per cent, and with a predominantly agricultural economy field crops had swamped all buffer regions and were now pushing into reserved forest areas. With a growing number of people living next to the forest and dependent on it for their building and grazing requirements, the attempted introduction of a domestically-raised predator was bound to be unpopular. The experiment would be opposed by many, among them those who, out of ignorance, considered that animals of wild origin which were hand-reared by men automatically lost their innate fear of humans.

Attitudes toward tigers tend to be extreme. On the one hand, there are people who accept the sensational accounts of Corbett and Anderson which depict the tiger as a man-eater, ever-ready to attack humans. On the other, there are the sentimentalists who try to make out that human killings are all accidents caused when people stumble upon sleeping tigers in thick cover and get mauled as a result. The truth in fact lies somewhere in between. The tiger with his trigger-sharp senses is seldom taken unawares, and when this does happen his first thought is to escape. He avoids man as far as possible. When he does attack humans, it is almost invariably because he is driven by expediency through, for example, a need to protect the young. But once roused, the tiger is a devastating killer with armament which no man can withstand. He is basically a predator however much the natural instincts are restrained by fear of the unfamiliar and the unknown, and when he moves in he moves with a purpose.

Since this was to be a first experiment, I realized that failure would have adverse repercussions and, depending on the nature of the failure, such an experiment might never be allowed again. (Khairi, a tigress in Orissa, had also been hand-reared, but she was treated as a house pet and had become so imprinted that her return to the wild was unlikely.) I had read about the lions reared by Norman Carr and George Adamson which had apparently deliberately killed men.

Admittedly, social animals such as lions are inclined to be more aggresive, but the tiger inhabits dense forests and thus might be more responsive to his environment. The question remained whether the initial experiment should be made with a male or a female. My feeling was that a female, with her more tractable and dependent nature, would be an easier subject. It also seemed likely that in a park which already contained a viable population of tigers, a male would suffer more aggression from the others.

All these factors had to be carefully considered before embarking on the project. Once I had resolved to go ahead, however, I realized that despite the self-searching there had never been any doubt in my mind that I would try to put a tiger back in the wild. There had been accidents with my leopards, and though they had not been to blame one-sided reasoning had cast them in the role of villains. Naturally, with my reputation of caring more for animals than for humans, my tiger experiment was bound to provoke an outburst of emotionally-motivated hostility. Nevertheless, I decided to press on regardless, sustained by the conviction that once I had the tiger with me at Tiger Haven the battle of the future would be a holding one, whereas if I became enmeshed in red tape I would never get out of the tangle, let alone get a tiger.

My first option was to seek help locally. The government of my home state, Uttar Pradesh, had political pressures on its doorstep and was unlikely to sanction such a project. Although the chief wildlife warden, who was a good friend of mine, was personally very keen on the idea and in fact would have been willing to start an introductory experiment of his own, I realized that the opposition of his political bosses could place him in a very dubious position. Besides, forests and wildlife were no longer the concern of individual states; they were now dealt with by the central government which had a more objective outlook on the subject of wildlife preservation.

Accordingly I wrote directly to the Prime Minister, Mrs Indira Gandhi, who, among her many preoccupations, had shown a particular interest in the wildlife of India and who had so readily set the stamp of approval on my leopard project by giving me two cubs. Her response was characteristic: I received a letter from her secretariat saying that the Prime Minister had approved my project and they were now engaged in the pursuit of tiger cubs! However, the search soon appeared to enter a period of bureaucratic doldrums and no tiger cub was forthcoming. Other countries had so exploited the breeding potential of zoo tigers by removing their litters at birth and hand-rearing them that there was now a surfeit in foreign zoos. In the land of their origin, however, many zoos had either all males or all females and reproductive activities were naturally at a standstill.

Some months later Dieter Plage, a cameraman of Survival Anglia, happened to show a film on gorillas to Mrs Gandhi. The Anglia Television crew had shifted part of their filming activities from Africa to India and were keen to make a film on the tiger as well as my leopard project. During the conversation after the film Dieter Plage was asked whether he could help in finding a tiger cub. At the time he was on his way to London and soon after, to my surprise, I received a letter from him saying that three tiger cubs, two males and a female, were awaiting my collection. The condition, of course, was that Anglia should be allowed to film the experiment of reintroducing the animals to the wild. Though the prospect of such an association was personally tempting, the logistics involved were so discouraging that I could not help but decline the offer, and the cubs were sent instead to Antwerp and the Bristol Zoo. Twycross Zoo, where they had been found, was asked to let us know when a female of the next litter would be available.

So it was that in July 1976 I came to England and hurried to Twycross to see the cub with whom I was to live on intimate terms for

4

some considerable time. Judging from my experience with hand-reared female leopards, which had come into season though without conceiving at the age of two and a quarter years, I guessed that a tigress would start taking an interest in the local tigers between two and a half and two and three-quarters, when she would perhaps be ready to opt for life in the wild. However, the same conditions did not apply: the only male leopard within about 160 kilometres of Tiger Haven was the one I had released into the forest, but at least two male tigers and three tigresses inhabited the immediate area. The unknown question was how these local tigers would react to an imported sub-adult with no blood relationship. After all, free-ranging tigers seem to stand a modicum of inbreeding and much of their mutual tolerance is due to familial recognition.

When I arrived at Twycross I was introduced by the owner of the zoo, Molly Badham, to John Voce who had hand-reared the little tigress. As we approached the cage in which she was housed, we heard the joyous hoots of the siamangs as they swung from the dead branches in their cages, and I could not help thinking of the gaiety these sounds must have lent to their native forests before the human hand reduced them to silence through commercial exploitation. Tara (or Jane as she was then known) was in a small cage connected to a large wired-in enclosure where she could be exercised. She was three months old and like most young animals had a most attractive expression on her face. She seemed devoted to John, who fed her morning and evening and took her out for exercise before shutting her back in her cage. He let her out of the enclosure and, after greeting him affectionately, she briefly climbed onto my head before being returned to her cage.

The first meeting had passed off well but I decided to spend three or four days with her so that she could get used to me before I took her away. It was lucky that I did, because the next time I went to her she promptly bit me! This hostile behaviour continued and in the morning after she had greeted John she would try to give me a nip, repeating the attempt during our walk. I was determined not to discipline her in any way until she got to know me. Once when I entered the enclosure alone she chased me onto a small table which was fortunately close at hand, after biting me on the forearm. Blood was flowing freely – by this time my trousers were more holes than trouser and my legs were covered in bruises. I therefore decided to spend as much time as possible close to her, and after our morning walk I would sit outside her cage and stay there until closing time. I was quite mystified by her attitude, since none of the three leopards which I had hand-reared had reacted in such a hostile way. I tried to persuade myself that she was playful, but the severity of her grip belied this, and eventually I concluded that my foreign smell was partly to blame. Also, she had spent most of her time in a cage without any companionship in spite of being hand-reared, and knew only John. Cats are nervous animals and their first reaction to a strange situation is hostile if they cannot escape.

Forcing the pace by adopting a dominant role would merely have aggravated the situation so I decided that patience was the only way to win her trust. My first step was to dedicate my torn pair of trousers to the cause so that she could get used to my unfamiliar smell. These now remained permanently in her cage, while I spent the whole day sitting outside it in a small wired-in passageway. Zoo visitors seemed to look upon me as some strange and lesser-known exhibit and, from the way they peered at me, I am convinced that some of them came specially to discover whether I was human or animal. On the third day Tara responded by rubbing herself against the wire netting on which I was leaning. She also indulged in *prusten,* a friendly noise peculiar to tigers which they make by exhaling through closed lips. I knew then that I was over the hump, and when I fed her in the evening before leaving I sensed that she was now more reconciled to this strange person who had come into her life. On the fourth day I consolidated my gain and by the time I left, although I had a few scars, I was confident that the worst was over. We were now ready to travel together.

Before we could leave, however, an ominous rumble came in the shape of a telephone call from India. Some bright person had pointed out that no zoos had pure-bred Indian tigers and that a mixed strain should not be imported into the country. I was taken aback and obtained confirmation from Twycross that Tara was indeed a tigress of Indian parentage. It struck me as a most ludicrous scientific quibble when every effort was being made to save the tiger from extinction.

While we were prepared to talk of racial integration among humans and condemn Hitler's theory of *herrenvolk*, it seemed that we applied different standards to animals which had the same natural functions as our own, but from whom we were too proud to take lessons. Also, India had been unable to produce a tiger cub for the occasion!

By now I had the bit firmly between my teeth since I realized that if I did not take the cub to India with me, I should never get it there. Fortunately the noted conservationist Dr Bernhard Grzimek had become interested in the project and had generously offered to present the cub as a gift to Mrs Gandhi; I was certain that his scientific reputation would carry the day. So I returned to Twycross to collect Tara and take her by truck to the home of Colin Willock (executive director of Survival Anglia) near Heathrow. When I arrived I found Tara shut up and, as I watched her pacing up and down the narrow confined space of her cage, I could not help but feel thrilled at the prospect of introducing her to a new life. Molly Badham saw us off, accompanied by her favourite chimp, and after a four-hour journey we arrived at our destination where Tara was lodged in an empty stable. She appeared rather bewildered by this rapid change of scene, and did not eat but climbed on top of me to show that we were now in this adventure together. Inside I met Dudley, Colin's Jack Russell terrier, who, though he had never seen a tiger in his life, avoided going near the stable for some days after Tara had left.

Early the next morning we set off for the airport where the authorities were quite enthralled to see this young tigress returning to the land of her origin. All formalities were completed in double-quick time and we loaded her into the baggage hold of the great Pan-Am jumbo jet. There seemed to be a lot of luggage in the hold and I was anxious in case the crates damaged the cage and hurt its nervous little occupant if we hit an air pocket. We therefore fastened the cage to one of the struts and with the assurances of the air hostess took off. Our first stop was Frankfurt where I was allowed into the hold followed by two hostesses, one with water and the other carrying a jug of powdered milk. Tara seemed to be standing up to the trip very well and drank some milk. I was thankful to observe that no heavy piece of luggage had rolled on top of her cage. There was a change of crew here and the kind hostesses departed after giving me some

7

champagne in the first-class lounge, leaving me once more, as I thought, to the mercy of the elements. The relieving crew were, if possible, even kinder and at Teheran Tara and I once again disrupted the passenger service. Soon the intercom was announcing our imminent arrival at New Delhi – here, I thought, my troubles would be over now that I was back on home ground. Little did I realize that the mills of bureaucracy had already started grinding.

At the airport I was met by a friend and an official from the Delhi Zoo where Tara would remain in Customs bond until the various formalities had been completed. It was a great comfort to be able to lodge the young tigress in the sympathetic atmosphere and comparative freedom of the Zoo instead of leaving her at the airport to be stared at in her small cage. I had imagined that my business with the Customs would take no more than a few hours, but once inside the lowering portals of the bureaucratic jungle my illusions were soon dispelled. It was to take fifteen days and the help of many friends before we were finally free to leave, and long before then I was wishing that Tara and I could change places – at least for a little while.

Official response to Tara's arrival varied according to the individual. Some people, learning that I had jumped the gun and returned to India with a tiger cub, went on an extended tour of far-flung outposts. Others, condemned to spend the best years of their lives in the stucco-fronted monstrosities where they worked, advised me to be patient. Sticklers for the rule of law suggested I send the cub back, get the necessary formalities completed and then arrange for its return. Some offered me tea and small talk. Others saw me out of their offices by the simple expedience of disclaiming any responsibility for the situation. At one point I was informed that I would have to pay Rs.16,500 (approximately £880 or $2,000) before I could take the cub away.

The final hurdle was the import licence. The gentleman who had to sign this document was due to retire within a few days and had many other calls on his time besides doing his job. We eventually ran him to ground after three days and, after gravely studying us and the paper which he was supposed to sign, he asked for a pen. A friend who was with me made the tactical error of producing a very handsome one, apparently of considerable value. As the official's hand hovered over

8

the paper, we leaned forward expectantly and breathed sighs of relief when he actually signed it. When my friend asked for his pen, which by this time was already in the licensing officer's pocket, he cast us a malevolent glance, threw the pen on the table and told us to return in the evening. Needless to say, he never came back to the office that evening, but I emerged the next day triumphant that my troubles were now behind me at last.

In the meantime, while I was feverishly rushing around, Tara had been having a much more restful time. She had a cage to herself at Delhi Zoo, with a large enclosure attached and a special assistant called Babu Lal to look after her. At night she was put into her air-freight carrier and locked up in the animal dispensary, but she did not seem to mind the sick and noisy lion or the old white tiger who was dying. Her diet was altered to buffalo meat and, as a concession to the drastic change in environment, she was given boiled water containing antibiotics. Morning and evening I came to take her for a walk. The mornings were the most exciting because there were no visitors about. We would pass the cage of the striped hyena who was usually not visible, but whose presence was indicated by the stench from the remains of his meagre rations. Then past the warthogs, whose attractive ugliness and quicksilver movements seemed to appeal to Tara. On to the jaguars who stalked and somewhat alarmed her, and the mountain lion whose plaintive squawk she did not mind. She had many visitors but, with her penchant for tearing loose clothing, they all watched her playful antics from outside the fence. She was increasingly learning to retract her claws, but was still inclined to nip and scratch when she became excited or noticed something strange. One day when I went to her wearing rather better clothes than usual after visiting some friends, she promptly – with the perversity of her race – ran at me and tore my clothing. She always greeted those she knew with great leaps, executed at remarkable speed, which sometimes alarmed people especially when she grew heavier.

Eventually, when all the bureaucratic formalities had been completed, the time came for us to leave. It was the middle of September and the days were turning hot and humid, so I decided to set off at four in the morning in order to complete the eight-hour journey by midday. We were up in good time but the fates had not completed their pranks and, when we tried to lower the rear door of the station wagon, I found it had jammed. It took some time to get hold of a locksmith and when we finally left it was after five o'clock. All went well until it started getting hot and sticky around ten o'clock, when Tara began to squawk. We stopped to give her some water and set off again when she had calmed down. When we were a little over half-way there I gave her a light meal but, from now on, progress was slower and with frequent halts we arrived at Jasbirnagar, not far from Tiger Haven, in time for a late lunch.

Tara had abrasions on her nose and on the sides of both eyes where she had rubbed her skin against the wire mesh. She was thirsty and on edge and promptly wound her head round the tree to which she was tethered; when I went to untie her she bit me. I now dismissed the station wagon in which we had travelled from Delhi and loaded the cage into a jeep trailer for the last lap of our journey. Only when the car had left did I discover that it had taken the shredded trousers which had served me so well, but hopefully I would need them no longer! The floods had not yet subsided and the approach road to Tiger Haven was under water, so I arranged for Sitara the elephant to meet us at the ford. We loaded the cage onto the elephant, crossed the river at what came to be known as Tara's Crossing and arrived at Tiger Haven. The great adventure had begun.

# Chapter 2

# Introduction to Tiger Haven

Tiger Haven has been my home for over twenty years and perhaps I should explain where it is and how I came to be there. The place itself is a small agricultural holding bounded on three sides by a wildlife sanctuary called the Dudhwa National Park which sprawls in a rough rectangle beside the Nepal border. Along the southern boundary of the Park, on which Tiger Haven is situated, runs an escarpment rising between 150 and 300 metres above the plains. Below it is the junction of two streams, the Neora and the Soheli, which every year flood the surrounding meadows during the monsoon. Here, among the sloughs and marshes of the open ground, is the favourite summer and winter habitat of the swamp-deer. In early winter one may sometimes hear the stentorian bugling of the rutting stags mingled with the mating call of the tiger. Above the escarpment lies the deep forest of sal trees stretching away to the Nepalese border. It was in this area that I intended to carry out the experiment I had planned — returning to the wild the tiger cub I had brought all the way from an English zoo.

Tiger Haven is named in memory of my brother who died as a result of the Chinese war, and I discovered it in 1959. At the time I had been farming nearby at Jasbirnagar for fifteen years, but with an increasing sense of dissatisfaction. Cultivation was taking over at an unbelievably fast rate and the herds of nilgai and blackbuck which were common when I first came to Pallia in 1945 had vanished. The nights which had once echoed to the calls of swamp-deer and hog-deer now resounded to the shouts of cultivators guarding their crops and the boom of muskets as the slaughter of attrition in the name of crop protection took over. I was also influenced by the impending imposition of a ceiling on landholdings.

One morning I set out to look for some land nearer the forest and further away from the scramble known as land hunger. I had heard of Billahia, but only as a place where poachers went to shoot animals or steal timber. It was an area of about 1200 hectares, consisting mainly of marsh and waterlogged land formed by the backwaters of the Neora river which were contained by the high embankment of the railway line to the Nepal border. I crossed the wide marshy area on an elephant while my dog Pincha swam. Slowly, following the winding course of the Soheli, we moved towards the forest which loomed like a vast curtain in the distance. Along the river bank there was a belt of miscellaneous trees. Occasionally we came across small herds of chital, or a hog-deer rushing headlong from one grass patch to another. On our right was a lake known as Tela Tal, stretching parallel to the river until it dried up opposite the notorious Chorleekh, or crossing used by timber thieves. Red-crested pochards, mallards and other duck rose from its waters as we approached, while under the overhanging narkul the common coot skittered away to safety. Further on we came across a sounder (wild pig). All the time the overhang of the forest had been coming closer, and soon we were at the junction of the Soheli and the Neora. The tall sal trees standing on the escarpment towered more than 60 metres above us. If I didn't exactly stake a claim, I told myself, at least this was the piece of land where I would like to start farming all over again.

There was one major drawback, however. Every year the land was flooded for several months, making it almost impossible to reach. The only approach then was from the south by rough vehicles through waist-deep water, and this was the route used by various unscrupulous people who came there to poach and steal government timber. The owner of the land, who had himself engaged in these activities, had become disillusioned by the heavy floods and I soon persuaded him to sell. Once I had taken possession of my new

Tara, aged three months, with Arjan Singh at
Twycross Zoo

Tara aged five months

eaving Twycross Zoo for Tiger Haven 30 July 1976

Tara being loaded on to the flight for Delhi

The last leg of the journey

17 September 1976, arrival at Tiger Haven

Tara being rowed across the Neora River

Tara aged one year

property, which amounted to about 100 hectares, I resolved to call it Dream Farm because I thought that the soil had been so enriched by the riverain silt that I could look forward to bumper crops. My initial task, to work out the best way to reach the land, proved to be much harder than I had imagined and for the first few years I was constantly engaged in a battle against the floods. I built embankments only to see them collapse under the monsoon rains; I experimented by cutting a channel from the Soheli and installing a sluice gate; but it was only after five years of very amateurish flood control that I could claim any lasting success.

It is now the end of 1979, Dream Farm has become Tiger Haven and I have given up all pretensions of farming. Today Tiger Haven is virtually an extension of Dudhwa National Park. I sow about eight hectares of fodder grass for the grazing deer and the rest of the land has reverted to the state from which it was 'reclaimed'. Instead of the bumper crops I envisaged when I first arrived, I am able to watch chital come out to feed in the evenings and know that they are breeding better because of the improvement in their forage conditions.

Before leaving for England I had made preparations for housing the tiger cub when she arrived at Tiger Haven. I had put wire netting round the dining-room verandah and reinforced the cage behind the storeroom with chicken mesh. A couple of the upstairs verandahs had also been wired in because I was obsessed with the possibility that the local tigers might react aggressively towards the new arrival. When I had been experimenting with leopards this danger had not arisen because there were no local-born leopards in the immediate area. The first leopard I had released into the forest was called Prince and, with his climbing ability, he was safe from other predators. Nevertheless, after he returned to the wild he had succeeded in mauling a sub-adult leopardess on one of his visits to Tiger Haven. The enclosures I had now put up would protect Tara from such a risk during the hours of darkness; in the daytime they could be used to accommodate visitors who, from the safety of the cage, would be able to watch the cats as they moved about outside!

The immediate problem was to introduce Tara to my dog Eelie and my leopardess Harriet who still resided at Tiger Haven. I had no qualms about Eelie because I had already seen how quickly she had got used to the leopards. Harriet, however, was another matter. When I left for England to collect Tara, Harriet had two three-month-old cubs which she looked after like a wild leopardess in the forest on top of the escarpment. The Big Tigress, whom I mentioned earlier, had lost her own cubs and after roaming the area calling to her offspring had started taking an interest in the increasingly vocal leopard. So it was with great reluctance and a sense of foreboding that I had left Tiger Haven. As it turned out, my worst fears were justified, and by the time I reached London the cubs were dead. The mother instinct of the tiger who had lost her own cubs had been the cause of another jungle tragedy.

Because of these events I expected Harriet's reaction to Tara's arrival to be hostile, so I put a collar on Tara and shut her in the wire-netted cage. Eelie roamed around outside and at meal times they were fed together. On the third day they were taken out for walks on leads. Tara's natural enthusiasm was inhibited by the fact that she was on a leash, and all went to plan until the fifth day when she was released and the two animals sniffed each other cautiously. Eelie seemed excessively casual until Tara, unable to contain her exuberance any longer, leapt on the dog who retaliated by baring her fangs and giving the tigress a nip. The order of precedence was thus established and continued until almost the end of their association.

There remained the more delicate task of an introduction to Harriet. The leopardess now spent most of her time at Tiger Haven and, though she had given up calling for her cubs, she still occasionally crossed the river on some abortive errand of her own. When we had first arrived at Tiger Haven Harriet was on the other side of the river so, having shut Tara in the cage, I called the leopardess and sent the boat over to fetch her. She turned out to be up a tree from which she gave a modulated reply before running lightly down the bole of a sloping jamun to hop into the waiting boat. The air was still but as soon as she reached the boat she sensed that everything was not normal, and her expression became tense and hunted.

As soon as she was across the river she rushed up an amaltas tree and gazed at the cage where Tara was enclosed though not visible.

14

There she stayed for half an hour before descending to sit in the boat. When she found that she was not going to be ferried across, she swam back to the other side of the river and spent the night in the Escarpment Machan. Next morning I managed to persuade her to come over and take a bone, and this time she stayed a bit longer before returning to the other side. It was the second day she had not eaten, which demonstrates the mercurial reactions of the big cats. For although Harriet had not actually seen Tara, an acute prescience had informed her of a presence which had not only inhibited her freedom during her forest wanderings but had also caused the death of her cubs. She was therefore understandably withdrawn, and though Tara would lie down and bawl when Eelie snapped at her, her acceptance by Harriet would have to come as a natural consequence of events. I could not force the pace. As it turned out Harriet gradually reacquired her normal appetite and began to spend more time at Tiger Haven. I fed her outside Tara's cage and now the revulsion she had exhibited earlier on had apparently changed to indifference towards the cub's presence.

On the tenth day I released Tara; Eelie stood by as a mutual acquaintance. As soon as Harriet realised that there were no bars between them, she raced up a teak tree, then immediately came down, ran at Tara and gave her an open-mouthed roar. Tara rolled over and grinned submissively, but roared defensively when Harriet crowded her. Harriet seemed to be aware that this was a cub and tried to play with her, but now it was Tara who was nervous. When Harriet crept up and ran at her, Tara inclined her head in an ingratiating snarl before rolling over with a defensive roar as Harriet leapt lightly across her. I heaved a sight of relief: Harriet had not been collared for some considerable time and it would have been difficult taking the two animals out together if their meeting had not been amicable.

I soon started taking them for walks in the forest each morning and evening. In the past Harriet had not been interested in these excursions but now she suddenly tagged along, and it occurred to me that Tara's presence was the immediate cause. It was quite a mixed procession with myself in the lead followed by Eelie, Tara and Harriet usually in that order, but occasionally changing as one animal would decide to ambush another. Normally Tara was the originator in these

15

games, but she was still nervous of Harriet; when she came close in a determined rush or if the leopard happened to look round, Tara would stop and either pretend that nothing had been going on in her mind, or divert her energy into a leap on Eelie. As she had not yet started sheathing her claws, she sometimes received an unfriendly response there too, and would then try to trip me up by hooking her paw round my leg. She seemed to have reached the conclusion at a very early age that she was safe from reprisals so far as I was concerned: she knew that when all else failed she could always take liberties with me. The walk continued in this uninhibited strain with Tara as the moving force, and it was obvious that the other two looked upon her pranks as those of a wayward juvenile which had to be tolerated and even encouraged within limits.

On our return we all sat down for a breather. This interlude seemed rather meaningless to Tara who jumped on Eelie. When she was rebuffed she tried to climb on my head but Harriet, who was sitting close by, now ran at her and spanked her. Later on when Harriet had a cub I saw her discipline it in a similar manner when the cub tried to scratch me because I had nothing for it to eat. This made me conclude that even the leopard's withdrawn nature is capable of jealousy once one has gained its affection. Needless to say, one of the most satisfying aspects of dealing with animals is that when trust is bestowed, it is not withdrawn whatever the circumstances. Faith is only broken on the human side.

Harriet now started making advances to Tara, and the way she would go to sit near her whenever her restless temperament allowed showed that she was impelled by an inner motivation. Harriet's cubs had been born ten days before Tara and it seemed possible that her maternal instinct somehow associated this oversized infant with her own lost offspring. The maternal possessiveness which had driven the Big Tigress to pursue the leopard cubs after the loss of her own, probably also impelled the leopardess to adopt a progeny from the same genus. The reaction might not have been so positive in the case of a young hyena or wild dog.

Sometimes Harriet would try to persuade the little tigress to follow her into the forest, which at first Tara was too scared to do. She would cross the river and call Tara with a peremptory and staccato *aom,* quite distinct from her higher-pitched greeting of *aaom*. Later she encouraged Tara to give chase when she ran up a tree, looking round to see if the latter was following. Tara's crude attempts at climbing were in ludicrous contrast to the fluid movements of the leopardess and she soon fell off. In time her climbing abilities improved but, though young tigers will climb if necessary, their instincts are essentially terrestrial and after an initial spurt they soon return to earth. The perpendicular teak tree which Harriet would ascend in stages was too much for Tara and she never got beyond a certain height even though I tried to tempt her with pieces of gunny sacking held out of reach. A leopard will cling to the bark of a tree with its claws and stay motionless, then thrust itself upwards by sheer muscular strength. A tiger, despite the colossal strength in its limbs, will not do this — it is obviously an inherited instinct. Similarly the leopard will start to come down rear-end foremost, then turn round quickly to run nimbly down the trunk. The tiger invariably comes down tail first.

Tradition says that the tiger is by nature a warmer animal than the detached leopard. I hesitate to confirm this when I recall my relationship with Prince: how he used to climb on to my lap, how he would appear for his morning toast and how, even just before he left me, he would sit on top of my legs or with his body touching me, as if physical contact provided him with a sense of togetherness which he missed in his solitary existence. I do concede, however, that the tiger is capable of wider associations, albeit temporary, and to that extent he is more social. The friendly sound known as *prusten* is made only by the tiger, lasts throughout life and is probably necessary for those fortuitous gatherings. Leopards do not have the same need for a call of such frequency, though they do have one to indicate recognition. Tara had a special falsetto call of *ah-ah-ah-ah* repeated *ad infinitum* until Babu Lal or I appeared. This decreased as she became more independent, and the last time I heard a single *ah-ah* was when she stood at the Soheli bridge at night as a wild tigress before turning away. It is probably a cub or sub-adult call because I have never heard it in a zoo. Another tiger speciality with no leopard equivalent is the habit of moaning while rubbing their head and cheek against the object of their affection. This also appears to last from the sub-adult stage through life.

Our morning walks were the most important part of the acclima-
tization process I had planned for Tara and they usually lasted about
two hours. Harriet was now one of the regulars and she and Tara were
getting more used to each other as time passed. It was interesting to
observe how Tara became increasingly aware of the extent of the
liberties she could take with her two companions. Once she ran at
Eelie, knocked her down and grabbed her throat in a playful display of
future tactics. Eelie lay there kicking her legs in a desultory fashion,
but when Harriet approached and sniffed her neck before leaping on
Tara, the underdog thought this was too much and wriggled out of
her lowly position to rout first the leopardess and then the tigress.

In spite of her efforts to be friendly Harriet was careful to keep
physical contact to a minimum in order to avoid the chance of an
aggressive encounter which is always likely, given the volatile
temperament and formidable armament of the big cats. It is the ever-
present danger of aggression which makes a prolonged courtship so
essential a preliminary to the frequent act of copulation among these
animals.

Initially I restricted the walks to the south of the river. The floods
had not yet abated and there were pools and stretches of water
everywhere. The weather was still hot and humid and it was very
difficult to keep Tara from drinking the mineral-rich water from
mudholes which all animals seem to prefer to 'sweet' water. Also,
despite her English upbringing, she had inherited the tiger penchant
for sitting in water. After her walk she would be allowed to wander
about a bit under supervision, and on these occasions she often
brushed up her stalking technique by practising on the large water
buffalo which I usually had around as tiger bait. She would stalk the
stolid buffalo using every blade of grass as cover, but if the buffalo
turned round she would turn tail and bolt. Whenever she came close
enough to the grazing animal, who realized that, whatever her
nuisance value, she could do no damage, she would hook her paw
round the buffalo's leg in order to trip him up. This game of 'touch'
appeared to give her great satisfaction, as she would then sit down
with a look of triumph on her face.

It was now time for her to be shut up during the day and as she had
already eaten a morning meal before we started on our walk, all she

needed was some boiled water with terramycin. Although she had probably had enough during her walk, she continued to drink throughout the day. Her diet had been changed and she was now given finely-chopped buffalo meat and — instead of bone meal and blood meal — some vitamin and calcium drops as well as a pig bone which she, like Harriet, particularly enjoyed. She was also dewormed once a month.

I was acutely aware that the drastic change in climate and diet was likely to have some sort of impact on her health. It therefore came as no surprise when, one morning after her walk, she suddenly became listless. Her paws were very hot and she did not eat her evening meal. At night she defecated properly but the next morning her stool was loose and frothy and contained a piece of undigested fat. I gave her a dose of Streptorex, which I had brought with me from England, and took her for a short walk, but she worsened as the day advanced and her paws were burning. I put her into a room where she stayed all night. Next day she passed another lump of meat. She seemed somewhat better but was still hot and listless and off her food. The following morning she ate a little mince but the next day her temperature was up to 104°. I called in the local vet who gave her some antibiotic injections which brought down her temperature. Neither she nor the vet liked these needle jabs, but unfortunately I was not qualified to use a hypodermic syringe. I could only hope that she would not need any injections when she was older. By the end of the sixth day she had recovered, but it took her a little while to get back her appetite and her playfulness.

Soon we resumed our communal walks and I began to think of taking the animals across the river which was still fairly high and would have to be negotiated by ferry boat. Tara had not yet been in the boat and I had visions of a minor Noah's Ark capsizing in mid-stream. In the event she made her maiden crossing without mishap — another link had been forged in the little community of which I was the leading member. I felt like a modern St Francis of Assisi as I led the way down the jungle pathways which would familiarize Tara with the immediate three-kilometre range round Tiger Haven. Our excursions would also serve notice on the resident Big Tigress that a newcomer had arrived on the scene. It was four months since she had lost her cubs and I knew that she was nearby because I had heard her mating in the Tiger Copse a

19

few days earlier.

On these outings across the river we sometimes went as far as the turning of the Sathiana Road which led to the Dudhwa building complex. This would make me apprehensive because a few extra steps would take Tara into human habitation, a dangerous place where one of my leopardesses had once been poisoned. At other times we went to Tiger Well on the Sathiana Road and, as the pathway along the river Neora was still muddy, we came back the same way. After a while I estimated that we had established a range of thirty to forty square kilometres. With a good supply of prey animals this would suffice for a tigress while still enabling her to maintain a protective base at Tiger Haven. The rest was up to Tara, the tigers and the future.

It was now three months since Harriet had lost her cubs and Prince had started visiting her regularly about once a month. I could sometimes hear them spending a night together across the river. Prince would not stay in the vicinity for more than one night; quite often he would go off to the north which seemed to be a new extension in range as previously he had only gone east or west. This probably shows that in the absence of intraspecific competition a predator's range can be unusually large, limited among males, perhaps, by the number of females they feel capable of handling.

Prince's reappearance indirectly affected our daily walks. One night in October Harriet crossed the river and I heard her courtship wranglings with Prince near the Jungle Fowl Jetty. In the morning she arrived back with a cut angling downwards across her nose, and it seemed almost as if Prince had swiped her after her refusal to go with him. Later on I found a scrape and deposit which showed that he had made a meal of pork, then moved off north. Harriet was not in a very good humour, but after a dab of iodine was ready to go out and we set off in an easterly direction. All went well until Tara chose to trespass on the leopard's familiarity by ambushing her and leaping on her back. This time Harriet quite understandably knocked the young tigress down and bit her, after which we all returned home very demurely.

Tara was growing rapidly and every day seemed to make a difference. She called less often when she was left alone and even stayed out one night in mid-November when we were unable to catch her after her evening meal. The waters had now subsided and our walks included visits to Leopard Haven where I was considering making an enclosure on the ground floor to shut her in for the night. This would give her a better feel of the jungle and also isolate her from visitors who kept coming in uninvited, disrupting her mealtimes and generally upsetting the routine which is so essential when dealing with animals. I tried to explain to them that I was conducting an experiment in rehabilitation and that, if Tara became too accustomed to having people around, there was a danger of an accident when she grew up and, if that happened, they would be partially responsible. However, I do not think this line of argument appealed to many; I used to hear all sorts of complaints about my arbitrary ways, and one visitor from Calcutta even went to the extent of writing to the newspapers.

We were now regularly crossing the river together by boat, and by the middle of December Tara had outstripped Harriet in size and thickness of limb. She had overcome her initial fear of the forest and would readily follow Harriet there. Often when I went to look for them I would find Harriet sitting near the small tigress or on a branch just above her. Here they would spend much of the afternoon. One day in December when we all went for a walk towards Leopard Haven, Harriet seemed lackadaisical and preoccupied and parted company from us at the Double Storey Machan. I did not see her for the rest of the day, but that night snarls and growls from across the river proved that Prince had once more put in an appearance. She must have been aware of his presence that morning.

Though Tara was very affectionate towards people she knew, she was nervous and aggressive with strangers. I am sure this was an individual characteristic, possibly due to her confined cubhood, which does not apply to all tigers. One day some Sikh friends came to lunch and Tara was shut in a cage behind the storeroom. She looked very appealing as she crouched demurely watching these gentlemen in their gaudy turbans drinking beer. The more they drank, the more insistent one of them became that she should be released. So eventually I let her out, hoping she would bite the insistent *sardar* in his red turban who, buoyed up with Dutch courage, asserted that she could not do much harm. After looking somewhat bewildered, Tara went

21

up to another Sikh and tore his shirt. The chances were that eventually she might have got round to the offending visitor but the odds were too great and I would have been very unpopular. In the event she became so excited that she bit me on the forearm as I returned her to the cage, where once more she resumed an innocent pose behind bars.

# Chapter 3

# Cubhood to Young Adult

On New Year's Day Tara 'sprayed' a mixture of urine and scent for the first time − on my legs: she had served notice that she was growing up. She would now wander about on her own at times, though as yet she had never gone very far. She continued her habit of tearing clothes, and the tattered condition of my shirts became an object of comment among the employees of the Forest Department. If threatened she would sometimes retaliate by getting up on her hind legs in a 'southpaw' stance rather like a boxer inviting one to come on. It was all done in fun, of course, but confronted by a 68-kilo animal with long sharp claws, one could be forgiven for misinterpretating her motives.

It is a moot point as to whether I should have disciplined her more in order to discourage these rough-house games. Knowledgeable people maintain that obstreperous cubs are disciplined by their parents, but I do not believe that this function can be taken on by a human surrogate. Only a true parent can judge the significance and appropriate context of a disciplinary act, and human interference can have adverse repercussions later on in life when an animal's very survival will depend on trigger-sharp and uninhibited reflexes. It can make the difference between feast and famine if the contained rush of a hunting tiger is conditioned by the subconscious recollection of a regular thrashing. I therefore think that I was correct in reducing my domination to a minimum even though I did have to bite the dust on occasion.

It is another matter with circus animals which are conditioned by fear. Clyde Beatty, one of the most successful lion-tamers in the world, claims that every one of his tigers and lions would have chewed him up if they had not been restrained by a built-in fear. My own experience could not have been more different and, when Tara rubbed her great head against my waist, I felt there was no reward as valuable as having gained the affection and trust of such a magnificent creature of the wild.

Tara's growth rate progressed steadily and I increased her meat ration to three kilos per day. We continued our morning walks which were really the only form of training I could give her. In other words, all I could do was to help develop her natural instincts. I encouraged her to walk ahead of me because I could both observe her reactions and also keep her from jumping on my back. One day when we were on our way to Tiger Well with Tara in the lead, she suddenly smelt the ground and then turned round, jumped on me and bit my bare legs. A distinct disadvantage humans have in dealing with the big cats is that a bite or scratch which leaves no mark on the fur of other animals is liable to damage the tender skin of a human. When I reached the spot she had been sniffing I saw the square tracks of a male tiger and, as we followed them down the road, she jumped on me twice more. This behaviour was probably an example of redirected aggression, born of insecurity and nervousness at the recent passage of the male. She did not react so strongly in the case of the tigress, nor did she roll at the site where the tiger had been as she did in the case of the tigress. This indicates a fine distinction in the tiger's sense of smell which is not generally accepted.

As January drew to a close Tara developed mange, a heavy infection which caused a sour smell in her fur and an unnatural stink in her faeces. She was also losing fur and sore patches appeared on her bare skin as she scratched incessantly. The local vet gave her various medicines but these seemed to do no good, so I wrote to the Chief Wildlife Warden in Lucknow who was kind enough to send the Zoo veterinarian. His diagnosis was a fungoid infection, together with a heavy infestation of worms which accounted for the foul smell in her faeces. Though tiger scat usually has a much stronger smell than a leopard's, Tara's was particularly offensive even by tiger standards. That this condition should have occurred despite regular de-worming was all the more depressing. However, the smell returned to normal after a strong dose of Stovarsoll. The skin infection was more resistant and difficult to treat because one had to be careful in taking liberties with Tara. We could not get her to submit to regular baths with a strong disinfectant and had to rely on a local application which she generally licked off, causing her to froth at the mouth in a most alarming way. She was also made irritable by the interminable irritation and consequent scratching. Despite these trials she still enjoyed her walks; indeed, it was while she was in this condition that she made her first kill, a baby chital who became entangled in some creepers when her group fled. Tara immediately climbed a tree with the small carcass to escape the importunity of Eelie who soon arrived on the scene, and there in due course she ate everything except one hoof. The next day she and Harriet found a dead monitor lizard with which they played and then rolled on in turn before losing interest.

I now started taking her further afield in order to develop her hunting instincts, but she did not like the cage built into the back of the jeep and had to be coaxed in with a piece of meat. When I let her loose in view of some 200 swamp-deer she stalked them quite expertly up to a point and then started chasing them. The thunder of 800 hooves, the clouds of dust which billowed out of the drying soil, and the falsetto alarm shrieks of the hinds and young males, orchestrated with the deep booming bass of the big antlered stags as they milled around in the tall grass — this was a most impressive spectacle and one which seemed to appeal to Tara's aesthetic sense for she continued the merry-go-round time after time interspersed with short periods of rest. The *barasingha* also seemed to enjoy it and galloped around in circles instead of putting distance between themselves and their pursuer. Sometimes Tara liked to vary the game, especially in the case of single animals, and when I tried to stalk with her she would leap on my back from the rear!

Tara's mange gradually disappeared and her temperament became more equable as the constant scratching subsided. Eelie developed a few small spots but they cleared up after a bath with Tetmasol soap, whereas Harriet who had a minimal amount of physical contact with Tara never got it at all. Nor, thankfully, did I; I have often wondered whether a drastic change in diet could induce a skin condition in animals. Eelie had developed a virulent mange after she was taken off the streets and other ill-nourished pups have reacted in the same way.

As March wore on Harriet started going across the river more frequently and would 'saw' when she detected Tara or myself from the tree where she was sitting. This is a beckoning call with the female but, as Prince was also a regular visitor, it is not quite clear whether she was calling to Tara or because her time of mating was at hand – perhaps the latter. Harriet was still very attached to the young tigress and spent a lot of time with her. She was also clearly fond of me and would greet me after an absence and search for me if she happened to come around; but she never behaved like a domestic animal. At this time she was spraying frequently both in the forest and at Tiger Haven. The fact that Tara had outstripped her both in size and weight did not seem to affect their relationship. They still went into the forest together and it was usually the leopardess who sought out the tigress for Tara was still nervous.

One morning Tara sprayed in the verandah and called softly twice. I had already noticed when she was ten months old that her deciduous canines were getting worn and uneven. She was approaching another milestone. She would take an interest in animals she saw on her walks but usually gave chase instead of stalking. Naturally this approach got her nowhere. Her new canines now started appearing alongside the original ones, nature's way of not depriving an animal of its essential equipment. As the new teeth developed, the roots of the old weakened and lay supine behind until, at ten months and twenty-one days, she had her first developed canine. Soon the others appeared and by the time she was one year old she had a complete set. Her appetite also put on another spurt, and she now splintered and demolished the pig bone she was given daily to strengthen her jaws and boost her calcium intake. Eelie, who used to have a symbiotic share-out in the marrow, now had to relay on Harriet who was increasingly absent from Tiger Haven.

Towards the end of March Harriet disappeared with Prince and stayed away for three nights and four days. Then one day we heard her returning as we walked towards Leopard Haven. Her vibrant growling, a sign of receptivity, soon subsided but she was now noticeably disinterested in Tara who for her part avoided the leopardess. Harriet had become receptive eight months after losing her cubs.

At about this time there was a political upheaval in India which, quite apart from its profound national repercussions, seemed for a while to threaten the cause of wildlife in general and my tiger project in particular. At a general election in March 1977 Indira Gandhi and the Congress Party were defeated by a motley coalition of opposition groups who combined to form the Janata Party. Ninety per cent of the electorate rejected Mrs Gandhi because of her crash programme of family planning, harshly implemented by sycophantic executives. A vastly overpopulated nation had opted for bigger families! Ironically, Indira herself was defeated by a person who was known as the clown of the legislature and who was rewarded with a ministerial post. The country which had hailed a divinity after the Indo-Pakistani war, had exorcised a demon. The western democracies welcomed the triumph of the democratic process which had already divided the globe into two warring camps by the rule of dogma, and now sought to blandish the third world. A triumvirate of aged politicians took over, each obsessed by a vaulting ambition to be Prime Minister of India. *Vae victis* — and the witch hunt was on.

In conditions of instability and political unrest the first casualty is invariably wildlife. For a time it looked as if the subject of forests and wildlife, which had at one time been a concern of the central government, would be returned to the State legislatures. However, the move eventually failed partly through the re-emergence of Mrs Gandhi as an effective leader of the

27

opposition and partly through the new government's impatience to carry out its programme of reforms.

Meanwhile I went to Delhi in search of new allies and hopefully applied to see the minister who had been so helpful in getting the Dudhwa National Park declared a sanctuary in 1969. He was now number two in the ruling triumvirate but was too busy to see me. Fortunately a politician who had been a distinguished civil servant before his retirement assumed, out of personal conviction, the chairmanship of the Indian Board for Wildlife. We had found a champion!

Back in my own district a host of people sought to exploit the new political climate to the detriment of the local wildlife. Some forest contractors made an application for the resumption of commercial forestry operations in Dudhwa National Park, claiming that since the Park had been the creation of Mrs Gandhi her downfall would not be complete while it survived. Many forest officials agreed, and a dawning fear possessed my mind that though I had applied for official recognition of a tiger introduction project, this had not yet been sanctioned by the State authorities. My fears increased when I learned that a group of people had written to the local political bosses claiming that a hand-reared tiger was a potential man-eater since it had lost its fear of humans, and that it therefore should not be allowed near a populated area. Prominent among the applicants was a man whom I had caught stealing timber!

I went to see the senior Forest Department official who was also in charge of wildlife and mentioned that I sought recognition for the tiger reintroduction project which had been approved by the former Prime Minister. Told not to mention Indira Gandhi, I said I had not done so; I was now willy-nilly drawn into the political vortex and this time on the losing side. The official, otherwise a good friend of mine, advised me to get the local M.P. on my side. Fortunately he also was an old family friend and we were able to have a long talk. However, knowing the strange bedfellows which politicans make, I redoubled my prayers that Tara should behave herself in the coming years.

She was approaching her first birthday and in the middle of

A walk in the sal forest in Dudhwa National Park ...

and on through the elephant grass

Arjan Singh and Tara playing, closely watched by Eelie

Eelie's turn for a game

Harriet the leopardess and Tara

Camouflaged in the jungle, aged eleven months

April 'sprayed' a properly diffused jet for the first time. It was about then that I received a report from my *filwan,* the man who looked after the elephant, that he had seen the Big Tigress sitting outside a patch of ratwa grass on two consecutive days. I made a quick calculation and concluded that she had cubs. I fed her with a couple of baits and hoped she might move her cubs further afield and away from Tara's normal circuit since wild carnivores do not keep their young in one place for very long for safety reasons.

By now the weather was getting hot. I partitioned a third of Tara's night cage into a shallow tank which was filled with water from the crocodile tank every evening after she had had her meal. I also thought it prudent to lock her up for the three hours in mid-afternoon when the staff broke off work to cook their food, and for this purpose I excavated a small reservoir in the original cage behind the storeroom. The cage had been designed for Prince, my male leopard, when the locals were after his blood, and had at one time also housed a pair of wolves. I now lined it with sand from the river and filled it with water, and Tara was left to her own limited devices for the afternoon. After a couple of days she decided that it was more pleasant to sit in the shallow river with its shady trees and flowing water. The big cats seem to have an ingrained intuition which informs them what you want them to do − then they do the opposite. This makes me conclude that they possess an instinct which prevents them from being guided by routine which would inhibit their freedom.

As the river bed in which Tara normally sat was only about fifty metres upstream of Tiger Haven, I was not very concerned but decided to keep a weather eye on her activities. It was lucky that I did. One afternoon when everyone else had retired for a siesta and I was sitting in her night cage (which I used as an office during the day), I heard two defensive roars from the other side of Junction Bridge. I emerged with a shout and saw Tara running towards the bridge with the Big Tigress in pursuit. Tara ran up the slope past me while the Big Tigress, spotting me, turned tail and bolted. I chased her down the road but she soon disappeared by turning right and crossing the newly-built Leopard Bridge. I went back and called to Tara, who after a while appeared looking sheepish but unmarked, and sprayed a nearby tree in an apparent release of tension. She had been sitting in the water under some jamun trees when the Big Tigress had come along the far bank, crossed over a fallen tree and entered the water in order to chase Tara up the opposite bank. She had obviously become aware of Tara's presence from her increased spraying, and had come to see her off her range in which she now had cubs to defend. I was lucky to be present because tolerance outside the family circle is based on the balance of power, and Tara was only a year old. Next day she was subdued, apart from being extra affectionate and demonstrative. Later on she turned back from her walk towards the Twin Lakes.

Tara was never really keen on car drives, and when she grew too large for the jeep cage I had another built onto the trailer, nurturing visions of tandem hunting expeditions with the three animals. However, man proposes . . . one day I put a weighing machine into the cage, which wobbled so much that Tara thereafter refused to get into it at all. We therefore continued our training walks. The roads were all dry and this was the best time to get her acquainted with the range I had worked out for her, and which naturally enough had Tiger Haven as the radial centre.

Our first walk was across the river down to Am Chauraha and east from there almost up to the end of the Sathiana Road; then a right turn into the Copse past Juliette Point and Prince's Monsoon Machan, and back over the river at the new bridge on the Neora. The next day we would go to Tiger Well on a western turn from Am Chauraha down to Chorghatia (or Thieves' Crossing) and then along the river back home. Some days we went as far as Kawaghatia. On others we would walk west to Leopard Haven, south into the meadow and then back over the Soheli via the Chorleekh crossing. To the east we would go as far as the metalled road. I estimated that we covered in all a nucleus range of about thirty square kilometres which Tara seemed by now to know well, judging from the way she often branched off on errands of her own and returned in her own time. Since her encounter with the Big Tigress I had a man stationed within earshot the whole time, armed with a tin, with instructions to bang on it if there were sounds of a fight. Tigers, like all other wild animals, are alarmed by a sudden burst of unfamiliar sounds, and even Tara would react to a tin banging, a device I often used to induce her to toe the line.

The walk via the Twin Lakes was probably the most interesting. Once we left the main Dudhwa-Sathiana Road, we would probably meet a herd of chital at the Jungle Pool. Tara would watch them with great interest without doing anything about it, and once she sat within twenty metres of a large herd and watched them for about half an hour until they moved off. Further on we would come to the Twin Lakes which were in the process of drying out. Here we usually found a mixed flock of resident comb duck and cotton teal, all busily feeding in the shallow water. Sometimes, stalking among them, there would be a solemn pair of black-necked storks which with their black and white plummage, black heads and long beaks, looked for all the world like a couple of invigilators at an examination among the industriously dabbling ducks. Having put them to flight, Tara would try to enter the water. She was usually put off by the squelching mud however, and would instead start chasing Eelie, then probably jump on me as I led the way through a patch of long grass past a machan kill site where later I was to photograph the tiger who became known to me as Tara's Male. We now came to a bend in the river at the Kill Ford where a big marsh crocodile lived in a deep pool before the Ford. As we approached he would slither gently into the river. The sand was firm and cool and Tara and Eelie would play in the water or chase each other up the steep bank. Eelie now looked very fragile compared with Tara who was remarkable for her lack of aggression considering that even in childish games the bigger boy usually chases the smaller one!

After spending some time here, we would move into the Tiger Copse where Tara once killed a fully-grown peacock sheltering in some tall grass. Despite encouragement she would not eat it, probably because she did not know what to do with the feathers. My leopards, on the other hand, always knew instinctively and would settle down to pluck the birds. Our path then continued past Juliette Point to Prince's Monsoon Machan where we usually found chital licking minerals from under the roots of trees growing on the edge of the escarpment. We sometimes varied this walk by following a deep-water channel in the forest where we might come across a barking deer licking salt from the bank. Our arrival would be greeted by a staccato bark, then the deer would run up the bank with what seemed like a chattering of castanets; this sound must have come either from the deer's hooves or his teeth which include two prominent tusk-like canines. Once we came upon two sloth bears digging a termite nest – they fled one way with a startled 'woof' while Tara fled the other.

On our walks to Leopard Haven Tara would from time to time take a dip in the river and I worried that she might meet other tigers doing the same. I had a pathway built through the thick undergrowth along the bank, and occasionally she would wrestle me down the bank and into the water. She appeared to have a very good strategic sense and would wait until a dip in the pathway placed her above me. I was only just able to hold my own and wondered how Milo of Croton shaped up with the bull calf which he was reputed to have carried until it grew up. Tara was more gentle with Eelie and would run at her and either swerve at the last moment or jump over her back. I now noticed something striking which became increasingly pronounced as she grew older; this was the way her paws used to thud, in contrast to leopards who run silently. The disparity was so evident, even allowing for the difference in size and girth of limb, that it may be nature's way of intimidating large prey. The leopard, on the other hand, hunts smaller species with sharper reflexes and thus needs to function more stealthily.

One of Tara's favourite play points in the forest was a bend in the river beyond Leopard Haven. Here a large asna tree whose roots had been eroded by floods spanned the water and the shade of numerous trees kept out the hot rays of the sun. The water was shallow, the sand cool and there was the thick trunk to walk across. Inevitably I was drawn into Tara's aquatic games as the indefatigable tigress tired out the ageing Eelie. Crouching in the water with her mischievous eyes glinting and just visible, she would suddenly launch herself at me with the same carefree abandon that she demonstrated as a cub. Once she made a wild leap from at least three metres and, though I was prepared, I fell over in the soft sand. I was left wet and gritty and forcibly reminded of the fact that Tara was growing up. My attempts to find out her weight had been a failure but I judged this at nearly eighty kilos. When she tired of her games in the river we used to move on to the meadow, and here we sometimes came across a herd of swamp-deer. Often Tara seemed to take only an academic interest in them, either because the deer were too big or too numerous for her, or simply because it was too hot. But a pig or a hog-deer was a different matter and Tara and Eelie would take up the pursuit in canine fashion, usually with no result. I sometimes wondered whether Eelie's influence on Tara in her formative years had affected Tara's style because she would never take cover.

The visits of the Big Tigress continued across the river where she would spray and roll and scrape, and often her scats showed that she was living well on a mixed diet of pig and chital. It was clear now that she was gunning for Tara. For her part Tara was spraying further afield and rolling where the wild tigress had rolled, though she would not scrape which, as I said earlier, seems to be a more mature form of symbolic aggression. Whenever she failed to return with us in the afternoon I posted a watchman armed with a tin on the escarpment.

Towards the end of May great thunderheads started to build up over the Nepal hills and occasionally storms with high winds swept the forest. During one of these storms a male tiger walked within twenty-five metres of where Tara was lying up and, as chital called in the copse, he crossed the road close to the Junction Bridge and continued over the river. Full pads of pugs with smallish toes showed that this was a young adult. Thereafter his visits became more regular and it was fairly obvious that Tara's presence was interesting him. She would now roll where he had rolled before her, showing her desire to get acquainted, but at the same time she was also nervous and kept jumping on me, though this behaviour was probably at least partly due to the coolness of the weather and the pools of water lying on the ground. When I slapped her she would dig her claws into my side, another sign of nervousness. Eelie used to resent this familiarity and chase her.

All the time the spate of visitors continued. Visitors were not particularly welcome for they always seemed to time their visits to coincide with Tara's meals, and once she was alarmed by strangers she would not come into her cage however great the temptation of the pig bone. One day a wedding party of thirty people arrived in a large van, and that evening we had the greatest difficulty in getting Tara back into her cage. As they left I heaved a sigh of relief and hoped that the happy couple had enjoyed their visit more than I had.

Soon afterwards a sleek limousine drove up containing an Austrian who claimed he made wildlife documentary films for television. He said he had been in the Park for two days and had not seen a tiger; I told him that some British forest officers had been thirty-five years in the country without seeing one! He appeared very insistent on filming Tara and would not take 'No' for an answer though I told him that this was a scientific project and that Tara was unused to strangers and liable to get excited and might even bite and scratch him and ruin his equipment. He returned three times and said he was willing to take the chance. Little did I know. That afternoon, in place of the Austrian, there arrived a young Canadian cameraman who had been committed *in absentia* to filming the tigress with all its attendant hazards. Tara seemed to smell foreign blood and promptly jumped on him and tore his shirt, scratching him at the same time, while he tried to fend her off with his movie camera. The young man, who had never seen a tiger at such close quarters, was thoroughly alarmed and fell down while Tara hooked a claw into his trousers. Luckily this drama took place next to Gran's Cage, and I held her off while he was bundled unceremoniously into it. As he drove away I could see that he was white and shaken. I do not know what passed between him and the Austrian producer on his return to the Rest House, but when they drove past me in Pallia on their return journey to Delhi, the cameraman got out to apologize for what had happened. The producer stayed in the car.

# Chapter 4

# Monsoon Adventures

In Northern India the hot season before the outbreak of the monsoon lasts roughly from mid-April to mid-June. Westerly winds build up during these two months into a searing and dessicating furnace which blasts the parched grassland. Only the river valley retains its greenness, protected by the tall salt trees whose perennial freshness is renewed by yellow-green leaves as they are shed. Occasional thunderstorms from the Nepal hills sweep down across the sub-montane forests, the high velocity winds broadcasting the sal seeds like a myriad miniature parachutes of an invading Lilliputian army. And after the winds come a barrage of hailstones.

However, the season has a peculiar fascination. The hot days are succeeded by cool nights which provide a respite for an exhausted world. Sloughs and pools, remnants of the previous year's floods, have dried out, and the only available water is from the river. All wildlife is concentrated along this green belt which meanders through dense woodlands and savannah. Here the tiger sits in the river to cool off and his prey animals come down to quench their thirst, their strident alarm calls often triggering a stampede as they scatter to seek other and less dangerous stretches of the river. At night the grazing ungulates crop the short grasses of the meadow and rest in the open as a safety

35

precaution against prowling predators. The rhythm of life and death continues. There is no heaven or hell for wild animals except the one created by man.

This particular year the rains were late but towards the end of June the wind changed to an easterly. Though cool and moisture-laden, the nights became humid and oppressive once the breeze died down. The swamp-deer herds which used to spend the hot hours under the noonday sun and the token shade of a solitary acacia now sought refuge in the forest from the vicious bites of the green-headed cattle flies. Even as fragmentary clouds drifted across the sky, Pandora's Box was opening as mosquitoes and stink bugs, leeches and scorpions came to life. It is one of those paradoxical quirks of nature that she tempers her bounty with a multitude of unpleasantnesses.

On 31 June the rains broke with unaccustomed violence, and while Harriet rested in an upstairs tenement of Tiger Haven for the last night of her pregnancy, the water bucketed down to the accompaniment of thunderclaps and brilliant flashes of sheet lightning. The river, which the previous evening had been no more than a torpid stream, was suddenly transformed into a torrent of liquid mud flowing down from the hills. There now occurred the local phenomenon known as *Uchhowa* when the river fish, their gills choked by excessive silt, die in thousands. As the water recedes – which happens very rapidly as it is soaked up by the parched earth – the gasping fish are left stranded on the bank to rot under the biting rainwashed sun. Predators eat their fill, the otters no longer competing with each other for the spoils, for there is more than enough for everyone. Brahminy kites wheel and swoop and egrets and pond herons sit contentedly on the banks. Soon, however, the windfall is over: an overpowering and ever-increasing stench pollutes the river banks as the rotting fish putrify and nature's scavengers are unable to consume the sudden bounty fast enough. After the first heavy showers there is usually a break before the monsoon proper sets in. These preliminary Gshowers vary in intensity and the local farmers maintain that the break in the rain is a respite granted by the rain gods to assist in agricultural sowings. But soon the parched earth is saturated and

January 1977. Tara, Harriet and Eelie at pla

Babu Lal watches as Tara playfully trips up Arjan Singh

April 1980. Tara, having now lived in the wild for three years, is observed eating a buffalo with her male companion Old Crooked Foot   (also seen below)

Summer 1977. Tara, Arjan Singh and Babu Lal.

the river rises until it becomes a steady flow of muddy water which will last for about four months. The grassy meadows where the local tigers have hitherto found shelter and shade are waterlogged, and the tigers seek refuge on the higher ground beyond the escarpment. This year the approaches to Tiger Haven were also flooded and Tara's routine underwent a change, for we now had to cross the swollen river and climb the escarpment into the forest before we could set out on our daily walks. The only means of making the crossing was by boat, and Tara had her own ideas about how this should be accomplished. After trying to wrestle Babu Lal or myself into the water, she would pretend that she was not interested in the expedition; but once we had boarded the boat she would land with a flying leap in the centre, nearly capsizing the craft. Eelie was then coaxed on board and very wisely sat stolidly in the centre until we reached the other side. Tara restlessly paced the boat and in her impatience she would lean her ninety-one kilos on the leading oarsman. This manoeuvre could easily have pushed one of us into the swirling waters, so we took turns in paddling while the recipient of Tara's body-weight hung on to the gunwales. Once we had reached the far bank, Tara would leap off the boat and rush up the escarpment slope, and it was only after she had disembarked that Eelie would step gingerly ashore. Sometimes we would entice Tara away from the boat while we rowed across in order to get her to swim. She was an exceptionally strong swimmer and no matter how swift the current, she kept a straight course. It was noticeable that she always swam with a rigid tail, often held outside the water and different from the leopardess who used her tail and rump in the swaying motion of a crocodilian.

In may ways this seemed to be Tara's finest hour of the day. Revitalized by a night-long rest and stimulated by the cold-water swim, she would bound down the escarpment slope, her paws thudding like a polo pony, and run at Eelie only to swerve at the last moment. With me she was less considerate and I would be the one who had to get out of the way. One day a cameraman crossed over with us. He had filmed Tara swimming the river and was walking behind me when I heard a familiar heavy thudding. I looked round to see him lying down in the same spot where he had just been standing; Tara meanwhile was already on her way up the slope. A camera was invariably an incentive for community games, and on one occasion when Tara was sitting down before the river crossing I tried to pose for a picture with her. As soon as she saw the pointed lens she rolled over, trapping my legs between her paws in a scissor grip, and brought me down on top of her. Her strength even now was phenomenal: the tractor-wheel weight closing the door of her cage, which required all my muscle power to shift, she would move casually with one paw. Her habits of ambushing and jumping continued and I again wondered how weaker people would put up with these playful ways.

As the monsoon built up and the waters closed in on Tiger Haven, the logistics of Tara's meat supply assumed formidable proportions. The district administrative authorities would not allow the slaughter of buffaloes in the area, so I had been sending for meat from 100 kilometres away. But now the approach road was flooded and the final stages of the journey had to be completed by an elaborate ferry system of boat and tractor, the latter replaced at high flood level by an elephant. Tiger Haven is surrounded on three sides by forest and the river and its spill waters make the humidity intense. It was therefore imperative to get the meat into the deep freeze as soon as possible, especially as the journey took about three hours and the packed ice gradually melted away. Often, having completed the journey, we found that the deep freeze did not work through a failure of the electricity somewhere on its long course from the power-generating station. Then we would have to start up the stand-by generator, driven by an ancient crude-oil engine whose massive fly wheel sometimes churned the muddy waters at high flood level in a spectacular fountain. Occasionally we wondered what would happen if the generator failed, but fortunately the sturdy old engine kept going and we were never put to the ultimate test.

We had several different routes for our walks on the other side of the river. Once on top of the escarpment, we would walk down Am Danda past Am Chauraha, turn left and keep going to Tiger Well. Alternatively, we would keep to the track until we had crossed the metalled road and then continue straight on; or we would turn left following the road and come back along a jungle track. Once we met some smugglers but, though we had plenty of firepower in the shape of Tara, Harriet and Eelie, it would not have been possible to harness it effectively, so we retreated. We often came across animals, especially on the road leading to Tiger Well where we sometimes encountered a solitary wild pig rolling in the puddles left by the rain on the motor road. Tara always seemed to be reluctant to chase the pig, but would follow when Eelie ran after it. Occasionally we came upon a sambar or a hind with fawn but, as Tara would insist on chasing them down the middle of the road, she got nowhere and they soon branched off into the forest with a metallic alarm call. The sambar's call is possibly the most reliable indication of the presence of a tiger, since often they do not bother to raise the alarm for a leopard.

Once we happened to meet a man called Khalid. Though normally I would wave all wayfarers to one side, this man (who was the gatekeeper at the Dudhwa Barrier) arrived round a corner unexpectedly and it was too late to divert him through the undergrowth: Tara, with the perversity of her race, would have been sure to investigate. Khalid was pushing a bicycle and I told him to walk slowly down the road while Babu Lal stood in front of Tara who was preoccupied with a bush on the side. All went well until he came opposite the tigress, at which point his nerve broke and he leapt on his bicycle and started pedalling for all he was worth down the road. Tara, who had finished inspecting the bush, thought that her hitherto dull companions had decided to enliven the walk, and promptly gave chase. She was decidedly faster than Khalid, and the crescendo of his cries rang through the forest as he pedalled furiously down the road. Finally he fell off into an outcrop of bushes whereat Tara, disappointed at what had originally promised to be a lively chase, returned to her usual companions. Later Khalid wrote a lavishly-worded complaint to the Chief Wildlife Warden in which he offered to resign his post.

Towards the end of June Harriet turned up at Tiger Haven after spending about ten days in the jungle. She was now heavily pregnant and behaved in a very aggressive manner towards Tara, who responded nervously and avoided the leopardess as much as possible. This change in their relationship was quite remarkable and showed an instinctive appreciation of the situation on Tara's part. On 1 July Harriet gave birth to a single cub. Tara continued to be on the defensive until the cub was weaned. I noticed that Harriet, after she had given birth, would roll in Tara's urine where it had trickled down an electic pylon in front of her night cage, and then urinate herself at the same spot. This habit appears to be part of the familiarization process which prevents nervous reactions leading to aggression. Normally it only happens between animals of the same species, but there would seem to be no reason why it should not be extended to other members of the family.

Meanwhile the Big Tigress continued to make her presence felt in a warning demonstration directed at Tara. Her visits were now more frequent and marked by an increasing amount of spraying, rolling and scraping. One afternoon early in July Tara let forth a defensive roar from a patch of grass which the flood waters had not yet engulfed. I ran towards the sound with a loud shout and saw her splashing through the shallow water towards me. She came over the bridge and rubbed herself against me, indulging in a few words of *prusten,* but did not appear unduly nervous. Investigation showed that the Big Tigress had approached her from the west where Tara must have seen her before running to Tiger Haven. A few days later the Big Tigress roared three times in the vicinity of Prince's Monsoon Machan to the east. The next day I happened to be away and Babu Lal took Tara and Eelie for their morning walk to the escarpment and towards Dudhwa. On the return journey he looked back to see the Big Tigress following them. When he shouted she vanished into the bushes, only to reappear a moment later. She was persistent and the shouts did not seem to deter her. Tara became very nervous but seemed to regain her confidence as they approached Tiger Haven. The flood waters were lapping the bottom of the escarpment and she went to sit down in the river. Babu Lal sat on the slope facing her, with Eelie between them. Suddenly Tara stood up, looked towards him and indulged in a nervous *prusten.* After a while Babu Lal realized that

40

she was in fact looking beyond him; turning round he saw the Big Tigress standing on the slope barely ten metres away. Seeing that she was observed, she grunted and bounded up the slope. Next day I went to investigate and found the pugmarks of the Big Tigress's cub, which seemed to be about four to five months old. They had come from the direction of the Twin Lakes, crossed the road and gone north in what was probably a shift of lair. The cub appeared to be the only one.

The day after that we went for a walk and once again saw the Big Tigress following us. When I turned round she quickly disappeared into the forest. On the road to Dudhwa we heard monkeys calling in the direction in which she had led her cub, but Tara gave no sign that the tigress was anywhere in the vicinity.

We decided to return to Tiger Haven but our adventures were not yet over for the day. When we were within a short distance of the Escarpment Machan Tara, who was in the lead, suddenly went into a crouch and moved rapidly opposite some dense bushes where she flattened herself at right-angles across the narrow path. I was about ten metres behind, followed by Eelie and Jackson with a tin can in his hand, deputizing for Babu Lal. Ahead of me I saw the tops of the bushes being agitated as some animal advanced towards the pathway. Tara was quivering with excitement: she raised her rump and swayed from side to side to maintain her balance in preparation for an attack. The bushes extended right to the pathway, and as the shivering fronds slowly came closer I caught a glimpse of a black object. It looked like a pig and I wondered what action the young tigress would take in the light of her previous reluctance to tackle one.

Suddenly the off-white snout of a large bear appeared and, to my vision from a slight angle, it seemed only a few inches from Tara's nose. There was no doubt as to who was the most surprised: the bear defensively half rose on his hind legs, changed his mind, then with a roar hurled himself at Tara who fled towards us with the infuriated animal in pursuit, looking like a runaway tank as his black bulk overflowed the pathway. I waved my stick and shouted and Jackson banged his tin and, just as I was wondering what I would do when the bear arrived in our midst, he veered and went

41

off at a right-angle followed by Tara and Eelie. Sensing that he was crowded, he gave a second guttural bark. Soon after Eelie reappeared, but Tara's self-respect seemed to be ruffled by her ignominious flight and she continued the chase for another half kilometre. As the bear turned, I noticed that the hair on his rump was missing; doubtless this skin complaint contributed to his bad temper that morning. A year later Jackson came across him again while he was sniffing some dead wood; looking up, the bear gave a grunt before lumbering off into the undergrowth. He seemed to be cured of his mange as Jackson reported that his rump was covered in hair.

Not long after this Tara had her first encounter with a porcupine. It had rained most of the night and by morning the river was rising rapidly when I took her towards the Croc Pool whose approaches were flooding fast. Jackson again accompanied us. On the way I found a porcupine quill and gave it to Tara to smell. She seemed inordinately interested and kept sniffing around until she located the rodent in a patch of grass. The only escape route for the porcupine was across the river, and it duly swam out and took refuge on the sloping trunk of a dhak tree. Tara followed and, catching it by its quill-covered rump, she flicked it towards dry land. I found her in a patch of grass with her paw on the porcupine which was still breathing. In response to my call she emerged with a quill sticking to the base of her throat and this I extracted; one in her paw she bit by herself. As she was reluctant to abandon the porcupine which was evidently injured, we left her for the afternoon.

On my return at about four o'clock the tableau had not changed: Tara sat in the grass patch with a frown on her brow, her paw on the porcupine which was still breathing. She came out when I arrived and hooked her paw round my leg as if to say 'What do we do next?' I think she must have been puzzled by the coat of quills. Eventually I killed the porcupine but, as Tara still kept picking it up and putting it down indecisively, we distracted her attention and pulled the carcass to Tiger Haven. She followed the drag scent into her cage where we placed the kill after disembowelling and skinning it. During the night she devoured the whole thing. At one point when Jackson approached her cage she snarled at him. This was rather surprising because he had been feeding her every evening, but in this case I think she was asserting a proprietary right to something she felt was her own. Also, although Jackson belonged to her clan, he was not close enough to be accepted unreservedly. When I went close to her she did not react in any way. I often tried to gauge the measure of her attachment by standing opposite Babu Lal, her regular keeper, on our walks, and found that invariably she would come and rub herself against me first in spite of the fact that he was the one who fed her. I am sure that such animals are aware of the degree of affection they are given; at any rate when Babu Lal left my service, it was clear that he did do without regret.

The porcupine episode seemed to give Tara's hunting instinct a concrete direction. A couple of days later a solitary langur appeared on a gular tree and started barracking both Tara and Harriet, who also happened to be present that day. He kept up a continuous commentary of coughing barks which Harriet, who was blasé by now, merely ignored. The monkey was not deterred by this display of indifference. Waiting for an opportunity when the two cats were out of sight, he jumped off the gular and with his long tail held in a loop over his back, lolloped up to an amaltas tree on the bank of the river. Tara's deadpan expression underwent a change and she swarmed up the amaltas faster than I have ever seen her climb. It was only by leaping from a height of nearly eight metres that the langur managed to save its life. Thereafter he raced to his previous mount where he remained until nightfall; it may have been my imagination, but his cough appeared to have assumed a note of querulous indignation.

Tara continued to grow apace and had now given up chasing birds, but she was very conscious of the presence of the Big Tigress who visited more or less every day. At certain places where the tigress had passed she would become aggressive. On our walks she often located pigs, sambar, chital and swamp-deer by her sense of smell. However, her unproductive habit of chasing continued. On two occasions she killed monitor lizards, using her paws to suffocate them, only to abandon the dead reptiles soon after. No doubt the lack of the hunger imperative influenced her wasteful habits. In the middle of August she killed her old acquaintance the solitary langur – whom she must have surprised – with her claws, and then rolled on it. Though rolling seems to be a habit of young adults and is often a prelude to eating, she left the langur in the forest. Perhaps it was not to her taste for it is a fact that tigers, like humans, do prefer some foods to others. Later that month she killed another monitor lizard, this time using her teeth, and on a different occasion she chased a sambar hind with a greater sense of purpose. Tara's hunting techniques were gradually becoming more sophisticated.

All the time I kept noticing slight behavioural changes as Tara approached maturity. She would indulge in *flehmen,* or wrinkling of the nose with a simultaneous drawing of the lips, protrusion of the tongue and slight opening of the mouth disclosing her canines. These mannerisms usually accompanied the sniff of a strong tiger scent, either her own or another tiger's. But I have also seen them when Tara was confronted by a pile of rotting fish and a dead and putrescent monitor lizard. She even used to confer this distinction on Jackson who was inclined to exude a particularly ripe odour on occasions. One day we walked down towards Tiger Well and came across the pugmarks of a tiger moving in the same direction. After a couple of aggressive leaps Tara followed me but appeared reluctant to go for her normal walk. She kept on looking back, and it was obvious that the tiger had gone down the road only a short while before. At the same time she smelt places of interest, grimaced and drooled, but did not roll as she did with the Big Tigress and was considerably more apprehensive. A tiger spray smells pungent even to the lay nostril, and to another tiger can provide information about not only the sex, but also the condition of maturity of another animal. On the return journey Tara strode back to Tiger Haven without loitering as she usually did or branching off into the forest.

As the days passed her nervousness at the menacing presence of the Big Tigress increased. Apart from the usual rolls and scrapes, the tigress had recently advertised her activities in the neighbourhood by killing a fishing cat. This act of wanton

On the banks of the Neora River

Tara in the Tiger Haven jeep

Sharing a drink

Climbing into a machan when about one year old

On board a 'dug-out' boat. Tara is nearly fully-grown here

aggression was obviously done to protect her cub, since no attempt had been made to eat the cat which in any case was too small a meal. The cat had been pursued down the road until the tigress caught and killed it, and had then been left lying on the roadside.

I sometimes feared the same fate might one day befall Tara, and soon events were to prove that my fears had not been groundless. Late in August I travelled to Lucknow to attend a wildlife meeting, and on my return I stopped the night at Sitapur. At 5.00 a.m. I woke up dreaming that I could hear distress roars from Tara which were getting fainter. I was running towards them but, as happens in dreams, I was getting no closer. I thought no more of it and at 7.00 a.m. left for Lakhimpur where I was to collect some meat for Tara. We did not reach the bridge site at the Nakauhwa, which was the terminus for motor traffic during the monsoon, until late afternoon. From here we were ferried across by boat over a gap which had been left for the construction of a bridge at some future date. The road had been started in 1962 after the Chinese invasion, as a means of repelling the Chinese army should they elect to come through Nepal. It had been completed a long time ago, but after seventeen years the bridges were still missing, and we were now content to regard their absence as a defensive measure which would delay the advance of an invading force. It also, more usefully, acted as a barrier for five months of the year against poachers illegitimately using the road as a means of entering the Park.

The Sarda river, which we passed before getting to Pallia, was in spate and the flooded Soheli waters were inching their way towards the metal road. The tractor had been unable to get through and the elephant was standing by to ferry the meat supply for the last lap of our journey. Fortunately I was bringing back so much meat that the crossing took some time. I had just loaded up and mounted the elephant when I caught sight of Babu Lal approaching with a somewhat crestfallen expression on his face. I sensed that some crisis had occurred and shouted to the jeep driver, who was getting ready to return to headquarters at Jasbirnagar, to hold on. My premonition had been correct: Babu

Lal informed me that Tara had had a fight with a wild tigress and had been badly mauled, but that he had managed to shut her up in her cage. Hearing this, I arranged for the elephant to make tracks for Tiger Haven with the meat while I recrossed the river, feeling rather sorry for myself after a long day.

We reached Pallia just after sunset and I went to the local vet to seek his assistance. He looked at the sunset, thought a while and then said he had to catch the night train to his headquarters. However, he allowed a subordinate to come with me and armed with hypodermic needles, anti-tetanus and tranquillizing injections we set off. We crossed the Nakauhwa and by the time we had walked about one and a half kilometres to the banks of the Soheli, where we branched off to the left, darkness had closed in. The water level varied from knee- to waist-deep as we splashed our way along the jungle path, guided by the stars and the gaps in the trees and fearful of stepping off the bank into the main stream. It was past eight o'clock when we finally arrived at Tiger Haven.

I found Tara licking her wounds and looking rather miserable but she gave me a welcoming *prusten* as I examined her injuries. Apart from minor scratches on her flanks, she had two deep wounds on the right side of her thigh and just off her anus. The outside wound was so deep and jagged that it was not possible to see the end of the contusion and the flesh appeared unconnected to the skin. The vet insisted that he would have to give her a series of three injections: sedative, anti-tetanus and antibiotic. It was left to us to work out how to adminster them. We noosed her with a rope with a sliding knot and Babu Lal held her head while I sat nearby, trying to shield the vet from her sight while he prepared to inject her rump. The first jab got through but prepared her for the second which she greeted with a loud snarl; somehow we succeeded in giving her the third shot. The vet was scared out of his wits but very bravely stuck to his syringe until it was all over. It was not nine o'clock but the problems of returning him to base seemed merely academic.

Later I was able to discover what had happened. It transpired that Babu Lal had taken Tara for a walk across the river and left her there as she would not return in the boat. According to my instructions, a man had been placed on the Escarpment Machan with a tin can which he was supposed to beat if he heard any strange noise, while the rest of the staff broke off for their afternoon recess. At about 7.00 p.m. there were sounds of a fight and roaring in two notes from the direction of the machan, but silence from its occupant; on being shouted at, he started to bang his tin and the noise of the fight, which was going on about fifty metres from the machan, subsided. Babu Lal and Jackson then crossed over and called to Tara who after a while came slowly out of the undergrowth.

It appeared that she must have been lying under a bush when the Big Tigress seized her. There was a trampled area and some hair with the splinter casing of a claw, which could only have belonged to the wild tigress because it was cracked and frayed. She had obviously taken advantage of Tara's recumbent and helpless position; it is doubtful whether Tara had been able to inflict any injury since the tigress had run away to the east as soon as the tin-banging started. When I asked the man in the machan why he had not banged the tin until he was shouted at, he said that he thought Tara was roaring by herself. I felt too irritated and relieved to inquire how he was so well-acquainted with tiger melodies. Tara had learnt the lesson that one should not sleep too soundly in the jungle – the catnaps of her forebears were an insurance for their safety.

She slept well and ate half her food the next morning, but was very lame and had to spend twenty-four days recovering in her cage. The Big Tigress did not visit for three days, probably because she was scared by all the shouting and tin-banging. Then she started coming again. Looking back at the catalogue of movements it is obvious that the local tigers and tigresses were fully aware of Tara's presence in their range.

# Chapter 5

# Maturing Senses

The summer rains gradually start subsiding in September and by the last ten days of the month they are over. The nights lose their intense humidity and become cooler, while during the day the sun — hitherto hidden behind dark monsoon clouds — blazes fiercely from an empty rain-washed sky. The river level recedes, and every succeeding day reveals a slight change in the colour of the muddy brown liquid until it becomes a light translucent green. Later on this hue takes on a darker tinge which lasts until the arrival of the next monsoon. Small fish begin a journey upstream and the junction between the Soheli and Neora seethes and churns with the splashes of the carnivorous catfish and the spray of minnows as they cascade out of the water in an effort to escape. By the beginning of October there is a touch of winter in the air.

Tara was now seventeen months old and becoming more independent as each day passed. She was spraying further along the range I had chosen for her, and the spray was more diffuse. She would also linger more often when I took her for a walk and make her own way back to Tiger Haven. This was all part of the process of familiarizing herself with her range. By now her eyes had changed in colour from dark brown to a light amber with a circle of green round the iris. She was increasingly aware of prey species though she continued to pursue instead of stalking them. And, as the weather cooled, she became more playful. Since she now must have weighed well over ninety kilos, I tried to discourage her from jumping on my back by all means short of disciplining her. I acquired a bamboo stick which I cut down the middle to produce a whiplike crack, but she soon got used to that. Banging on a tin was not much better. I tried to jump aside when she came to her final leap but that ploy only worked occasionally because I often mistimed my sideways movement or Tara anticipated it. I then tried running at her when I saw her crouching, and that sometimes did the trick. On other occasions her rush would start at the same time as mine and then it would depend on whose nerve broke first.

Though it would perhaps be anthropomorphic to ascribe a sense of humour to the big cats, it seemed to me that Tara had a certain elementary sense by which she delighted in the discomfiture of others. Whenever we went for a walk along the river, she would invariably try to wrestle me into the water from a suitable vantage point. If she succeeded in knocking me down the steep bank of the Soheli her pleasure knew no bounds. Once when I was walking down the escarpment she took a flying leap on my back; the impact of her weight sent me hurtling down the slope but fortunately I was able to grab a thin tree with one hand and went round and round with the momentum. As Tara galloped off with her tail in the air, I could almost detect the smirk which said, 'I will do better next time!' She would also come bounding down the escarpment slope at Eelie, and since the dog's back was too small to leap upon she would hook her large paws round Eelie's hind legs and try to trip her.

Meanwhile Tara's relationship with Harriet had undergone a complete change. Harriet's cub, which I named Mameena, had been suckled for three months and was in the process of being weaned. Tara had been studiously avoiding Harriet during this period but now, almost overnight, her attitude altered and she started to greet the leopardess with a nervous *prusten*. Soon they were sitting in the Copse together and chasing each other, and I marvelled at the subtle communication process which had evidently triggered this sudden change in behaviour.

As for the Big Tigress, her visits continued but uneventfully. I often found mud in the faeces which she had deposited on her scrapes opposite Tiger Haven. Perhaps this was the aftermath of weaning her cub, because Harriet also was licking mud and I noticed that mud deposits occur more often among females.

One day during one of our walks we came upon a school of ten otters in the river. Both Eelie and Tara ran to the water's edge while the otters milled around chittering and squeaking, sailing past like small schooners and occasionally standing up in the water to have a clearer view. After a while the two animals tired of the spectacle and we continued our walk. On the return journey Tara disappeared near the Croc Pool but I thought no more of it as she would now often break off on some errand of her own. However by the evening she had not come back, and though chital called in a patch of sugarcane close to Tiger Haven, a prolonged search did not produce the errant tigress nor did she respond to our calls.

By next morning I was concerned since she had never stayed away like this before, and a search party consisting of Babu Lal and Jackson went out to look for her once more. At about 10.00 a.m. she was found close to the spot where the chital alarm calls had been heard the previous evening. She had pairs of small fang marks on the side of her mouth, on her elbow and under her armpit, as well as on her flank and back, and for a while I was mystified as to the reason. At first I suspected a fishing cat but gradually it occurred to me that the otters were responsible. Tara had obviously remembered where they were and had returned to deal with them on her own. It seemed that she had ambushed one of them and, with her reluctance to use her canines as an offensive weapon, had sat upon it. Thereupon the other otters must have ganged up and bitten her, forcing her to release their companion.

This was borne out one day in December when Tara caught one of a school of eight otters who were crossing an open stretch of ploughed field. The other seven promptly surrounded the tigress and stood around chittering petulantly while Tara looked from side to side, all the time grinning nervously. I am convinced that they would have attacked her once again but for Babu Lal whose

51

appearance on the scene frightened them away. This was the first time that Tara had used her canines; but though she took the dead otter into a patch of grass, she did not seem to like the fishy smell. She visited her kill on two subsequent mornings but it was merely to remove it to other sites and thereafter she lost interest.

As winter drew on we found it increasingly difficult to shut Tara in her cage in the evening. Without the inducement of a pig bone it would have been impossible, but even so the operation was not easy. Babu Lal devised a noose with a running knot but the problem was getting it round her neck. She would crouch behind a bush and run at the noose-holder, hoping to knock him over. Sometimes we would offer her a bone and wait for gluttony to get the better of her before slipping the noose over her head. At other times she would pull loose and run away with the noose dangling from her neck. This could have been dangerous because if she had encountered other tigers, she would have been at a physical and psychological disadvantage. Once we had the noose in place, we would bang a tin behind her to get her moving.

One day chital called feverishly at nightfall in the large field which had been prepared for wheat sowing. We had been unable to locate Tara earlier in the evening and now it was apparent that she had been lying in wait for the chital, who with the onset of darkness had come out into the safety of the open field. I turned a large searchlight on the field and picked out the numerous pairs of eyes of a herd of chital. Behind them was a single pair of eyes, infinitely more luminous and changing in colour with every alteration of angle from light green to a smouldering red to the hot-white radiance of an electric bulb. The chital galloped round in a circle amid a chorus of girlish alarm yelps while Tara bounded after them, frequently pausing to regain her breath for the big cats are unable to sustain a burst of speed for any length of time. All the participants seemed to be enjoying themselves, even the chital who made no effort to escape. I got into a jeep and with Babu Lal carrying the noose, we drove into the field and switched on the headlights. The entire tableau was now outlined in relief, the only variation being the shadows which lengthened and foreshortened as the animals swept across the lights of the advancing jeep. At last the tempo of the game slackened and, blinded by the glare of the headlights, Tara walked up to us with a *prusten* and Babu Lal was able to slip the noose home. The next evening she stayed away from the headlights and we had to leave her bone in the cage in the hope that I would hear her return and be able to shut the door before she once again decamped.

One morning in the middle of November she gave four fully mature tiger calls on being let out of her cage, and was very frolicsome on her walk. After our return she went to the copse across the Junction Bridge to spend the day, as I thought, in a patch of grass. About three o'clock in the afternoon I heard loud distress calls. It was fairly obvious that they came from some variety of deer but, obsessed as I was with the aggressive posture of the Big Tigress, I ran towards the sounds in some trepidation. I was soon overtaken by Eelie who was also on the way to investigate and she entered the patch of grass behind which we could hear the cries. When I arrived on the scene I saw a small sambar fawn standing in the shallow Soheli stream where it had taken refuge, and Tara trying to pull it up on to dry land. I recrossed the bridge to the other side so as to get a better view and beheld the amazing sight of Eelie, who had now taken over, standing in the stream and nipping the fawn. Tara, meanwhile, had been driven out of the water and was running agitatedly up and down the bank. This was rather high-handed behaviour on the little dog's part and after I had tied her up, Tara once again entered the water and pulled her first kill on to dry land. Though she would probably have been able to deal with it on her own, I had the carcass disembowelled for I knew that she would stay with her kill until it was finished, and there was always the chance of other tigers appearing on the scene. The copse was partially surrounded by strips of white cloth which were originally intended to safeguard Harriet and her cub from prowling tigers, and now would hopefully perform the same function for Tara. She stayed with the kill all night and by the next morning had consumed one leg and part of the other in the conventional style of tigers, who begin eating from behind and between the thighs after having first bitten off the tail.

It is interesting to watch carnivores opening a kill: they first make a small hole at the prospective site of feeding with their incisors and later enlarge the orifice with their canines before beginning to eat. Thereafter they use their carnassial teeth, or molars, to masticate large gobbets of meat they have torn loose, doing this slowly and deliberately since their jaws have no lateral movement. I presume the tearing sound interspersed with the cracking of large bones that one hears when sitting over a kill comes from this process.

The next day Tara stayed with the kill and was very friendly and playful when I visited her. She ate snacks off and on during the day, but by nightfall word seemed to have got around because a tiger called persistently to the south. Later in the night another tiger, who was to become known to me as Long Toes, walked along the river on the far bank from the east and blasted off in a full-throated call opposite the place where I was in bed. I was jerked out of sleep by the sheer volume of the sound, and as I rose to investigate he called again further along the river. A visitor who had been ill for eight days was alerted into convalescence and felt much better the next morning! It was fairly clear that by some system of communication the local tigers had become aware of Tara's kill: Long Toes had actually walked up to the screen of white cloth before turning back, scraping continuously in exasperation as he went. Just how the tigers had become aware of her kill is a moot point. Tigers will often go off in search of their companions, and face-rubbings and sniffings presumably spread the news; but although this kill was localized one two separate tigers knew that it had taken place. The next morning Tara finished the carcass and returned to her cage. That night a young male tiger avoided the cloth by some devious means and visited the site of the kill.

It was about this time that Harriet brought her cub Mameena to Tiger Haven for a brief visit. We shut Tara up and when the leopard cub approached her, she retreated into her cage. This convinced me that she would not have harmed the cub. The next morning we released Tara and Mameena again came within five metres of her, but I was appalled at the difference in size and hastily led the tigress away.

54

The appearance of the male tiger at Tara's kill site was the prelude to a series of visits from him and the beginning of an association which was to have a powerful influence in drawing Tara back to the wild. She was already showing several signs of increasing maturity. One day when she saw a herd of chital she lashed her tail with a violent sideways motion for the first time, and I remembered that my leopard Prince had done exactly the same thing shortly before opting for freedom. Now the presence of a male tiger in the district was strengthening Tara's independent instincts. The tiger in question had the full pad but comparatively small toes of a young adult. The size of the toes in tigers and leopards develops after the pad growth has ceased and is a strong recognition factor between a young adult and fully mature animal; so too are the hind paws which appear narrower during the period of final growth, after which they mature as the hindquarters fill out.

By the end of December Tara was calling loudly after release in the morning. On one occasion she did not follow me as usual but went off across the Junction Bridge on her own, calling frequently and forcefully, towards the Double Storey Machan. In the evening she was found across the river at the base of the escarpment from where she returned, still calling continuously. This change in routine persisted and each morning she would go off on her own and roll where the male tiger had rolled. His visits had become more frequent and I decided to name him Tara's Male or TM for short. It was fairly obvious that the rolling was a process of getting acquainted, for Tara was also wandering restlessly up and down the escarpment. She still returned for the evening meal but would call loudly on her way back. To me it was clear that something was about to happen.

One day in the New Year when she was let out of her cage she made the usual beeline for the Double Storey Machan, calling as she went. Then she turned off into the grassland to the south where Babu Lal left her. In the evening swamp-deer raised the alarm opposite the Haldu Machan, and I went to the spot and called Tara. For some time there was no response; then she appeared from across the Soheli, came up to me, rubbed her head against my waist and moaned softly. I glanced at her left leg, which seemed to have a limp, and saw four slight fang marks on her forearm. At the same time a tiger roared in annoyance about 200 metres away: clearly Tara had been with him and he was now voicing his anger at her departure. I could barely restrain a shiver of excitement at the thought that she had rubbed against the tiger's great head only a moment before. Then he roared again as he moved away. Old loyalties and her feed habits had triumphed for the time being, but the bonds were weakening as the summons of her own kind gradually and inexorably took over.

After this incident her calling ceased for a while though she still went off on her own and returned later and later in the evening. One day swamp-deer called loudly near Chorleekh to the south of Tiger Haven and Tara rushed past her cage in a state of agitation. Next morning I found the pugmarks of a tiger and a tigress in a wet pitch of grass. Tara had come across comparative strangers, as the pugmarks belonged to the tiger known as Long Toes who was temporarily associating with the Big Tigress.

A few days later she disappeared for the day and when night fell she still had not returned. At about nine o'clock we placed her food and bone in the inner cage and I went off to have dinner. While I was away she sneaked into the cage and located her food, and by the time I reappeared she had finished her bone and eaten half of the seven kilos of meat she was now being given. She then went off to greet Babu Lal where he was cooking his evening meal. Since the bone was usually the means of enticing her into her cage I foresaw difficulties, particularly when Babu Lal came to report that she had vanished into the night after looking in on him. I wondered why she had not visited my bed which was next to her cage: hand-reared animals are prone to decamp with some familiar article if they cannot find the person for whom they are looking. Prince had done this with my lens case, Harriet with my shoes, and my two monkeys, Elizabeth Taylor and Sister Guptara, with my spectacles.

In the event Tara also ran true to form. After satisfying her immediate hunger she had torn a large hole in the mosquito net and removed my blanket, which she shredded in a mustard field fifty metres away. The half portion of meat which remained in her cage looked singularly unappetising and I wondered whether she would return to finish her meal since there was no response to my calls. A little after eleven o'clock I was woken by a *prusten* and saw, in the half light of a torch, an ingratiating face looking at me from about half a metre away. As I got out of bed, she made another pass at the net, but I managed to dissuader her; I then shut her into her cage where she finished her food. Next day I worked out that she had come down the escarpment from the Teak Plantation along the Am Danda and crossed the Leopard Bridge, whereas in the morning she had gone to the grasslands to the south.

Tara's movements were now becoming impossible to control as an inner compulsion drove her every morning into the forest from which she returned later and later in the evening. I was almost sure that she was spending the time with the male tiger. The only cubhood trait she retained was an inordinate fear of the man who cleaned her cage in the mornings. She would run and hide as soon as she saw him, and as he was highly unpopular with the rest of the staff everyone thought she was a very discerning tigress.

Since the end of the monsoon I had been thinking of further isolating her from humans, for though she would instinctively avoid strangers it was not difficult to imagine her becoming familiar with people as she grew in age and confidence. I therefore applied to the Forest Department authorities for permission to build an enclosure for her inside the Park where she would associate only with her two keepers. Bureaucratic procedures led to the inevitable delays and when they did give me permission I was told to take Tara to a different site which would have involved moving her to a location with which she was not familiar. Her range, after all, was around Tiger Haven where the local tigers knew her by scent and later by sight. In the area proposed by the authorities she would have to get acquainted with a new set of tigers. Strangers are not tolerated in tiger circles, and with her growing independence survival might be hazardous. Moreover, in successive years, one of the resident males there had killed a young tiger and an elderly tigress, both presumed to be from neighbouring ranges. So instead I resolved to renovate Leopard Haven by building a wire-mesh cage under the tree house. My intention was to keep Tara there for the night, with two men living upstairs. The Chief Wildlife Warden agreed to this and I started work immediately for I hoped to be able to shift her place of residence on 15 January.

In the morning in which I planned to move her, Tara called repeatedly before going off across the Junction Bridge and into a patch of grass on the way to Leopard Haven. The finishing touches were being applied to her new cage and I followed soon after to see when it would be fit for occupation. I had ploughed the field in front of the tree house and intended to sow some fodder grass and build a salt lick as I had done when Prince used to live there. On the way I met Harriet who started following us and a little later Tara also appeared. As we approached Leopard Haven they made no move to turn back. I was afraid that the carpenters working on the cage might be alarmed by their presence so I asked Babu Lal to take the two cats away, which he succeeded in doing after I had chased them. Harriet then returned with Babu Lal to Tiger Haven, but Tara branched off and, crossing the river, went up a ravine in the escarpment. At Leopard Haven I found that the carpenters had almost finished so I returned in the hope that the move could now go ahead.

However, by nightfall Tara had still not come back. I waited some time, then had dinner and went to bed. Her food was placed in the inner cage and a bowl of water left at the entrance so that I would hear her lapping it and then be able to close the door. At midnight I heard the sounds of an animal drinking at the water pump reservoir outside. It was a bitterly cold night as I got out of bed, put on the verandah light and with the bone in my hand called to Tara. At first there was no answer but as I glanced towards the door I saw her crouching below the steps, her eyes gleaming with mischief. Her hesitation plainly said: 'I want my bone but not at the price you are demanding.' Then she made a dart at me, knocked me against the partition and rushed out again. I put out the light and waited, and soon hunger got the better of her and she entered the night cage which I shut before returning to bed. In the morning she was up before daybreak and pacing her cage as she had been for the past fifteen days. On being released she called once and crossed the bridge.

That day I had to leave Tiger Haven to attend a meeting in Delhi, but Babu Lal relates that in the early night a bear grunted and fled near the Double Storey Machan and Tara visited the Jungle Fowl Jetty Reach. Her pugmarks showed that she came as far as her cage, though she did not enter it, and that she had then swum across the Soheli after jumping into the tethered boat. The next three days she spent with the male tiger in the neighbourhood: several places where the grass had been flattened by rolling revealed the presence of the two tigers. Then they disappeared – Tara had finally chosen to return to the wild.

Tara running away with Arjan Singh's hat at eighteen months

An abortive attempt at killing a domestic buffalo

Tara grimacing ...

and stretching

Heading for home, followed by Eelie

Tara indicating her presence by spraying, aged
fourteen months

Cooling off in the heat of the day

y before her return to the wild on 16 January 1978

July 1977, aged one year six months

# Chapter 6

# A Wild Tigress

According to my estimates Tara had jumped the gun and opted for free living many months earlier than I had expected. I had originally thought that she would retain some association with me until she was able to conceive at the age of three and a half, but it is true that this view had been modified by my experience with Prince who had chosen freedom when he was only two years old. But Prince was a male and males were supposed to become independent sooner than females; also, he had been living in the wild since the age of ten months with only brief contacts with the people he knew. He hardly ever saw outsiders and when he did, his first reaction was to remain out of sight unless he knew someone in the assembly. Tara on the other hand had spent her night hours at Tiger Haven, and though I had tried to insulate her against outside visitors as far as possible, this had not really worked. Moreover, one would expect a leopard with its shorter gestation period – approximately three months, against the tiger's three and a half months – to mature earlier than a tiger. All these factors suggested that one had to look elsewhere to discover the reasons for Tara leaving my custody at the early age of twenty months and ten days. The most persuasive explanation seemed to be that she was constantly aware of the presence of other tigers who were for their part increasingly conscious of her existence.

By contrast there were no other leopards in the vicinity for Prince to encounter.

It will be obvious that nowhere do I claim to have taught Tara anything, for the simple reason that a human cannot teach an animal: his lifestyle is too different. The tiger belongs to the hours of darkness when his acute senses are employed in a search for prey and for procreation; the daylight hours are devoted to the seclusion which he normally seeks. The human, on the other hand, lives in an artificial environment of his own making and it is sheer arrogance for him to claim that a hand-reared wild animal will be so smitten by regular mealtimes that it will not wish to leave. In reality, what Konrad Lorenz calls the 'Great Parliament of Instincts' governs the reactions of wild animals. For example, I have recently acquired a fishing cat which was abandoned when she was isolated by a grassland fire. Her name is Tiffany and she was about ten days old when we started to bottle-feed her. After a month she was put on a diet of minced meat. One day she went missing, and we eventually found her in a shallow stream dabbling industriously with her small paws looking for fish. Her instincts had taught her what I could not. Similarly, when Tara left she too was responding to her instincts: as a female she was more dependent than a male because of her biological functions, and what she did was to exchange one form of dependence for another, choosing as a replacement the young male tiger who had been in constant attendance in her later days at Tiger Haven. All I did was to give her the option and the opportunity. When people who should know better say that it is impossible to reintroduce hand-reared wild animals into their natural environment, they speak through ignorance. The instincts of such animals pull them towards a return to natural conditions of life, and all that is required in the case of major predators is that they should be isolated from humans soon enough for them to retain their inborn natural abhorrence of the human presence. Once necessity and the environment take over, the dependent animal will soon evolve into the complete predator.

I returned from Delhi a week after Tara had disappeared but there was no news except that she had been around with the male tiger, TM, for four days and had subsequently moved off to the west. This looked like the final parting and it remained to be seen whether she would be willing to retain a tenuous liaison with Tiger Haven, and also whether she would be able to remain on the range with which she had become familiar, for she was still a young adult and no match for the other tigresses in the area. It was only in such a situation that I would be able to follow her movements and perhaps aid her in times of stress.

For the moment however Tara seemed to be keeping her distance. I often went out with Eelie to look for her, calling continuously as I went, but there was no response despite the fact that her pugmarks revealed she was in the vicinity together with TM. On one occasion we found that she had followed us and some time later she was seen on top of the escarpment by a local range officer who claimed that she had run after him for a while. However, after three weeks the message seemed loud and clear: while remaining in the district, Tara had no intention of resuming a past relationship. Her attachment was to the range in which she had been brought up and to TM, her male companion.

It soon appeared that she had made her headquarters to the west of Tiger Haven, so I selected a site opposite the Haldu Machan and tethered a small bait with which I imagined she would be capable of dealing. This was quickly killed but the manner of killing was altogether too professional, and further investigation established that it had been done by the Big Tigress. Soon after this my cook Kharak Bahadur saw a tiger emerge from a patch of grass near Tiger Haven and move away to the north-east. It was too far away to recognize the animal so I walked towards the point where it had disappeared, calling Tara as I went. Jungle fowl continued to cackle in a field of sugar cane, showing that the tiger was walking away from me at an angle. As there was no reply to my call, I returned to the barley field the way I had gone and, happening to look round, saw Tara's male looking at me from about fifty metres away. For some time we stared at each other and then, while I continued calling to Tara, he slowly walked along the edge of the grass at an angle of sixty degrees. The fact that TM had heard me calling Tara and returned to investigate seemed to show that he associated Tara's presence with my voice. This raises an interesting speculation as to the degree of recognition which tigers in the immediate vicinity have of the men who visit their kill-sites, particularly as it occurred on more than one occasion.

Apart from Tara and TM there were a number of tigers on or visiting the range at this time. One of them was the male I had named Long Toes. Although they were involved in occasional scuffles over a kill, it soon became apparent that Long Toes and TM were prepared to share their meals, as I was able to observe on a number of occasions. Once I even witnessed TM sitting five metres from a kill patiently waiting his turn while Long Toes ate his fill. Also frequenting the range were the Big Tigress and the Toeless Tigress, an elderly animal with the toe of the left hind pad missing (possibly lost in a trap) who had her range to the west of Tiger Haven. Tara was frequently in the company of TM but it was difficult to assess the extent of her dependence on him for though their pugmarks were constantly seen together, she did not seem to visit his kills very often. In fact, I am inclined to think that during this period of transition when she was still instinctively dependent, she was nervous of the presence of Long Toes.

I offered a reward for news of her and as word got around that she was no longer in my custody, reports of various incidents began to come in. A neighbouring farmer claimed that she would not allow his labourers to harvest the sugar cane and would come and sit on the cane bundles. This proved to be untrue. I was then informed that she had attacked one of the man's buffaloes and was eating it alive. On going to investigate I found that the buffalo was dead and its spinal vertebrae had been crushed. Though this was not the orthodox method of killing such a feat denoted considerable power, and I promised to pay compensation if the culprit was my erstwhile tigress. I therefore dragged the carcass to a place opposite Chorleekh and the next night the Toeless Tigress followed the drag and fed on it. Needless to say, my neighbour did not agree with my view that Tara had been exonerated; indeed, in his eyes, my well-meant offer of generosity merely confined my duplicity.

Shortly after this Long Toes killed a man at Kawaghatia where a large number of buffalo carts and men had been stationed in prime-tiger habitat. These carts belonged to the Forest Corporation and were creating a disturbance in the Park. At first the cartmen tried to have the tiger declared a man-eater, and when they failed in this objective they stopped work and refused to remain in the forest. Eventually they were persuaded to stay at the Park headquarters, but when TM attacked one of their buffaloes near the Twin Lakes they finally withdrew, the rout was complete and everyone breathed a sigh of relief.

Meanwhile I continued my programme of tying up baits in the hope of luring Tara into the open. The baits were frequently killed by TM whom I saw on several occasions, but Tara remained elusive. The first opportunity of establishing her presence in the neighbourhood fell to Jackson when he was dragging the entrails of a carcass around a patch of grass in which we suspected she was hidden. While he was engaged in this task, a small tigress rushed out of the grass but unfortunately Jackson was carrying on a lively conversation with his assistant and was unable to identify her. Towards the end of March I came across one of Tara's defecations for the first time. It was an unhealthy yellow-green and contained mud and a few infant-porcupine quills. Since her buffalo defecations had always been semi-liquid, black and tarry, it appeared that she was still not sharing TM's kills on a regular basis. But despite the fact that she must often have been hungry, she never made any attempt to return to Tiger Haven.

Tara had now been living in the wild for almost three months and at this point an interesting change took place in the social relations between the local tigers. In the middle of April Tara's pugmarks were seen for the first time with Long Toes near the Ghulli Pool. Evidently she had switched partners. Not long after, this was confirmed when my brother Balram made the first definite sighting of Tara as he was driving towards Tiger Haven. With him was Kharak Bahadur who occasionally deputized for Babu Lal. As they crossed the forest boundary they saw a lean tigress coming up the river bank. She started towards a stretch of grass but when Kharak Bahadur had the presence of mind to get out of the car and call to her, she turned round and crouched, looking at him. Unfortunately Balram brought him back in the car to alert me instead of leaving him there to keep watch, and by the time I arrived with a plateful of meat there was nothing to be seen. I made Jackson climb a tree overlooking a patch of unburnt grass while I started calling, and soon Long Toes advanced into a clearing in the middle of the grass. I then put Kharak Bahadur up the tree and he confirmed that this was not the tiger he had seen earlier. Obviously that tiger must have been Tara, but it was equally clear from her refusal to answer my calls that she had no intention of establishing contact, and that her friendly advance had been entirely fortuitous. Though I stationed a man to keep watch for the remainder of the day and put out a bait at night, no further developments took place. This incident was primarily of interest in that it showed that Tara was alive, albeit thin, after several months of free living. It also confirmed a voice recognition by Long Toes, similar to the one by Tara's Male.

Meantime TM, who still shared kills with Long Toes, had also found a new partner. Early in May his pugmarks were seen coming from the Croc Bend to Harriet's Silk Cotton (a tree in front of Tiger Haven where Harriet spent much of her time), in the company of a tigress whose own pugmarks appeared similar to Tara's. The thick dust made it impossible to identify them definitely; all one could be sure of was that they did not belong to the Big Tigress. At first I thought this must be Tara, but that evening there was an explosive roar from a patch of heavy grass lining the northern edge of Tiger Copse. Thereafter the moaning whine of a male tiger climaxed by the defensive roar of a tigress continued throughout the night, highlighted by the strident shrieks of roosting peacocks as these periodic explosions of sound disturbed their slumbers. These were the unmistakeable sounds of two tigers copulating, a situation which I found confusing since Tara was still too young to breed. One possible explanation was that it could be a false heat. Some time later that night Long Toes arrived in the vicinity and from the constant swivelling of his hindquarters as he sprayed the outlying bushes, it was obvious that he was aware of the presence of the mating couple. But eventually he moved away without any altercation taking place.

This behaviour contradicted the popular misconception that males will fight to the death during the passage of an oestrous female. The fact that Long Toes was a more powerful animal than TM merely lent plausibility to the idea that finders were keepers, even among tigers.

The mating noises continued through the next night but we were unable to locate them. On the third evening, which my experience with leopards had taught me would be the last, I tethered baits at two points and sat down behind a grass screen on the river bank overlooking both sites. At about eleven o'clock a monkey called and a tigress appeared out of the grass on the river bank. I could have wept, for this was not Tara after all. The tigress that came into view was thin but had a longer tail and different markings. I christened her the Median Tigress, for I had not known of her existence until then. An interesting feature of these events was that neither tiger showed the least interest in the bait although they had been without food for several days.

After this disappointment I resumed my patrols in the forest, and though Tara continued to elude me I was constantly aware of her presence. One day, accompanied by Eelie and Harriet, I went to inspect a small jamun tree at the Leopard Bridge which Tara had sprayed the previous night. The spray was more than seven centimetres in diameter and nearly a metre off the ground. Eelie ran her nose up and down some blades of grass on which a few drops of liquid had fallen and looked up at the spray. A puzzled frown appeared on her forehead, she did a token urination on the ground below and moved away. Harriet then arrived, unended her posterior and planted some spray about fifteen centimetres below that of the tigress. Since this demonstration had been standard procedure after Tara had been let out of her cage in the morning at Tiger Haven, it seemed to be conclusive proof that Harriet and Eelie were able to recognize the tigress by smell after nearly four months of separation.

Soon afterwards I decided to tie up a small bait near the jamun tree at Leopard Bridge and this proved to be a good move. That night there was a thunderstorm and Tara came as far as the hand pump near the servants' quarters before going to a sandspit where the baits were watered. This was the closest she had been to the main building since she left Tiger Haven. She then went on to the Leopard Bridge where she made two feint attacks on the bait but, judging from the marks in the sandy soil, she seemed to have been put off by the buffalo's demonstrations. At the third attempt she killed the buffalo by seizing it at the nape of its neck. This form of attack is the most efficient since it paralyses the animal by crushing the vertebrae; but it may involve injury from the buffalo's horns and is generally only used by a powerful and confident tiger. Death is instantaneous.

Tara had made her first kill of a bait and she now broke the rope which held it and started to pull the kill towards the west. The initial momentum for dragging a heavy kill is usually by a series of jerks with the killer facing in the opposite direction to the drag. Then the tiger will turn round pulling, with the kill to one side or even between the forearms. This procedure may be repeated *ad infinitum* to clear obstacles like saplings until the tiger feels like feeding, but Tara jerk-pulled it for only about ten metres. When I arrived at the kill the next morning she had eaten about two kilos and, after I left, she came to eat a kilo or so more.

We probably made a mistake at this stage when we dragged the carcass several metres into the open, where we could see it from a hide near the Leopard Bridge. At one point Jackson saw Tara enter the water very briefly. Later on I took up my position in the hide while Jackson sat facing a bend in the river near the Double Storey Machan. I was hoping to get some identification photographs as there was still a great deal of scepticism about my claim to have succeeded in returning a tiger to the wild. It was very hot and the blistering sun shone relentlessly on the exposed hides. At about two o'clock Tara came into the water but opposite Jackson. He had a pair of binoculars, and after satisfying himself that it was indeed Tara he came and called me. I crept to the hide, camera in hand, but had not realized how close she was and could not prevent her from seeing my movements through the tattered screen. I saw her long enough to recognize her before she moved away up the bank. Then I made another mistake by not calling to her: after all, she had only retreated from the glimpse of a human form and she might have responded to my voice as she had to Kharak Bahadur earlier on. Nevertheless, I had at last succeeded in setting eyes on her.

As the monsoon approached and the weather became increasingly hot, I continued to use the Leopard Bridge site for tying up bait because I wanted to centre the scene of operations as close as possible to Tiger Haven. The main objective, of course, was to establish beyond doubt that Tara was now a wild tigress; but quite incidentally a great deal of interesting information was emerging about the social relationships of the other tigers on the range. Late in May I made a surprising discovery. TM killed a bait and then concealed himself nearby when Jackson arrived on the scene. The same night Long Toes moved off towards the east from Croc Bend, calling as he went. In retrospect these events were obviously significant, for not long after TM returned to the site of his kill in the company of Tara. She had changed partners again! Subsequent investigations showed that at this period she was associating with both male tigers. Tiger relationships are in fact much more flexible than is generally supposed. Tara had been able to shift her dependence to Long Toes when TM was mating the Median Tigress, and then move back to TM when he became unattached. Tigers also display a remarkable degree of tolerance when it comes to sharing kills, and on one occasion I discovered that no fewer than four tigers had fed on a chital stag killed by TM. This mutual acceptance of each other allows sub-adults and cubs who have lost their parents through accidents to attach themselves to mature animals as an insurance towards survival.

One day I found Tara's pugmarks leading into a patch of narkul near the Croc Bend and decided to tie up a goat there in the hope that its bleating would attract her. The goat, which had originally been imported for the benefit of Prince, had grown blasé over the years and after a few desultory bleats it curled up and went to sleep. Even its pungent goat smell did not prove sufficient to attract the tigress – perhaps she had strayed out of the patch of narkul. That night I was woken by a falsetto *ah-ah* which was the same as the welcoming call Tara had used for Babu Lal and myself in her early months at Tiger Haven. Thereafter there were two soft grunts and I got out of bed and called to Jackson; I imagined a buffalo might have got untethered but, finding nothing amiss, I went back to bed thinking that I must have been dreaming. However, in the morning we found Tara's tracks running down as far as the Junction Bridge where she had stood for a while. Then presumably hearing my voice, she had crossed the river. The Neora was very shallow at the time and she had sat at the edge of the Jungle Fowl Jetty looking towards Tiger Haven before climbing the escarpment and moving off towards the Teak Plantation.

In the middle of June the monsoon broke in earnest, causing a shift in the local tiger population. This shift is chiefly influenced by the flooding of the grassland pastures, the consequent scattering of prey animals and the fact that baiting more or less ceases during the rainy months. The Big Tigress and Long Toes moved to the west and north, and Tara and TM were the only tigers left in the area apart from an occasional visitor. The reason they stayed, I believe, was almost entirely due to Tara's compulsive attachment to the range on which she had been brought up. Also, I think her association with TM was more than one of mere convenience, for a mutual attraction does exist between two animals.

At first the flooding was not very intense and we used to find Tara's pugmarks – sometimes on her own, sometimes with TM – on all sides of Tiger Haven, though mainly to the east. One day I was informed by graziers that two of their cows had been killed by a tiger near the Ghulli. We went to investigate and discovered that the story was true; only one cow had been eaten and TM appeared to have done the killing. In the silted mud of the receding stream we found Tara's pugmarks as well, and noticed that vultures had started alighting to the south. A further search revealed a third small cow lying in the open among some bushes. This animal had been seized by the top of the neck and the neck itself was most efficiently broken, whereas the other two cows had been held by the throat. All around were Tara's pugmarks, but it appeared that after dragging it for a few yards she had abandoned her rather stunted and bony kill in order to share TM's prize cow.

70

As I have already mentioned, the killing technique used by Tara in this instance is one normally only indulged in by self-confident tigers. That she had again used this technique reflected her continuing immaturity, for the horns had been sharp and could have hurt her. As for the fact that three animals had been killed, this probably demonstrated (to use an anthropomorphic comparison) a desire to show off among the young.

About a fortnight later a small bait which I had put out at Am Chauraha was killed in the same manner, suggesting that Tara was again responsible. The sagittal crest of the skull had been fractured by a canine in the killing, showing that her grip must have slipped in the struggle. On the whole, however, Tara was not particularly interested in these buffalo kills; she usually left them to TM, and it was only in his company that she would consent to feed. This attitude seems to be shared by most tigresses: given normal circumstances and an area with a good prey base, they will often pass by a buffalo bait without attempting to make a kill.

During the monsoon an unexpected feature of the hunting procedures of TM and Tara emerged. Early in August the river overflowed its banks and there was nothing but a vista of water to the south of Tiger Haven. I had thought the tigers would confine themselves to the dry land on top of the escarpment while the floods lasted, but to my surprise I heard swamp-deer calling one afternoon to the south of the barley plot, and some hours later they were still milling around in the water calling frantically. Obviously there had been a planned and prolonged hunt by Tara and TM in the flooded grasslands. The two tigers had made use of the high-water level to locate their prey, whose movements were handicapped by their efforts to escape in the splashing water. A stalk which would normally be over one way or another in a very short time had been converted into a combined operation lasting a minimum of three hours and probably longer. It is no wonder that after such exertions the tigers should stay to finish the last vestige of food in preference to a stationary buffalo kill. For whatever is said regarding the absence of taste glands in the great cats, they do have food preferences. I am also inclined to think that the monsoon is not a pinch period for the tiger. Similar amphibious hunts are probably the rule rather than the exception, and it is likely that tigers move about much more than usual during the daylight.

At about this time I was able to check on the extent of the range within which Tara was operating. We discovered that one night she had completed a circuit of the Dudhwa Forest Rest House and met TM in a jamun copse to the south. From there the two tigers had crossed the railway bridge over the Soheli river. This was a very dangerous operation as there had been accidents in the past, but fortunately the railway engine which normally lay in wait for unwary cats did not materialize. The next night Tara's pugmarks were found on the Chorghatia Fireline leading to Tiger Well. From there she had turned east along the road, but branched off south and come along the bottom of the escarpment, passing the Jungle Fowl Jetty on her way towards the Monsoon Machan. Here she dropped a small black defecation containing a great deal of grass, some chital hairs and a blue-bottle which she must have scavenged during the hours of darkness when presumably even bluebottles sleep. Judging from these movements, her range appeared to cover between forty and fifty square kilometres and was more or less the same as the one I had introduced her to while she was living at Tiger Haven, though it was shared of course by other tigers and tigresses.

By the middle of October the approaches to Tiger Haven had begun to dry off and I moved the baiting site to the Croc Bend. At first Tara and TM kept to the west, but gradually they shifted operations eastwards and towards the end of the month TM killed a bait at the Bend. That evening the carcass was pulled to the Kill Ford, and at nightfall the tigers came from across the river where earlier sounds of squabbling had been heard. TM dragged the carcass into the river and up the other side, but finding the going rather difficult because of heavy sand, he took it back into the water and pulled it downstream. Clearly he had realized that it was easier to move the carcass with the help of the current.

Two days later I heard the nasal moan of a male tiger which indicates that sex is about to take place. Tara was only two and a half years old but I was not surprised because of my experience with the leopardess who had had a sterile mating at the age of two and a quarter. However, the process was considerably less tempestuous than the mating of TM with the Median Tigress, for though the nasal approach was present there was no explosive riposte from Tara, probably because she was still only a young adult. The sounds appeared to come from a small outcrop of jamun trees between Tiger Copse and the Twin Lakes. Closer investigation showed that the two tigers were located under a spreading haldu tree surrounded by a wall of grass. Into this grass they had dragged a kill, for it appears that tigers have no objection to eating as opposed to hunting during the mating process. On the third morning the tell-tale sounds seemed to move away north to the base of the escarpment, but this may have been due to the ventriloquist quality of tiger calls. At any rate that night they were back in the same place. On the fourth morning they eventually moved off for good, and when Jackson and I went to investigate we found that the mating site had been selected with great forethought. The haldu, which had a diameter of more than eighteen metres, was surrounded by a thick wall of grass but had only a few small, stunted bushes under its immediate umbrella. Here the tigers had spent a blissful three days and nights.

The kills were now being regularly dragged into the Tiger Copse grass, so I put up a machan on a nearby silk-cotton tree. The tree platform was about twelve metres off the ground and overlooked the whole immediate area. One morning I climbed the ingenious ladder which had been put up by Jackson and found that a kill had been taken a little way into the grass and mostly eaten. Suddenly five crows flew over what looked like a small clearing in the grass patch and returned to their perch on a jamun tree. As the object of their interest appeared to be some distance from the kill, I wondered what was attracting their attention, but when they repeated this manoeuvre three or four times it became obvious that they were watching the tigers. Although they were circling at the same height as I was sitting, the angle prevented me from getting the same view, but apart from saying, 'Oh, to be a crow', there was nothing I could do. Suddenly I heard an *ah-ah-ah-ah*

73

sound which though in a somewhat staccato key, was basically the same falsetto call which Tara used with me and with which she was now calling her tiger. This sound was repeated in a nasal note a few minutes later, but soon even the crows seemed to lose interest, silence fell and the tigers moved back into shelter.

Tara had now been out of my care for nearly a year and it was becoming increasingly difficult to recognize her pugmarks. It was therefore essential to get a photograph which would prove beyond doubt that the tigress in the neighbourhood was indeed the one that I had reared at Tiger Haven. The stripe pattern in tigers changes with growth and age but the cheek stripes and the eye spots, though asymmetrical, are immutable. Thus a photograph taken now could be compared with one of Tara when she was still at Tiger Haven and, if the two matched, the issue would be resolved once and for all.

With this object in mind, I shifted the bait site to the north bank of the river which was closer to the Tiger Copse grass patch and also more secluded. Over the next few weeks a number of kills were made both of wild prey and the baits I had put out. On one occasion, in following up a drag, we discovered that a tigress had sprayed six trees within an area of just over ninety metres. Thereafter the spraying had abruptly stopped. At the time I imagined that the tigress responsible for this interesting behaviour was Tara, but as we soon discovered this was not the case. One day early in the New Year, while I was away, Jackson and another man followed the tracks of the tigress and came to a small ravine where they saw a cub disappearing into some bushes. Simultaneously the tigress started to growl. Very sensibly, Jackson withdrew to the road as the bushes began to shake violently and then, with a series of coughing roars, the tigress rushed towards them in a demonstration which brought her to the edge of the road. Nervously they moved away, and a short while later she appeared on the road itself to see whether her behaviour had been sufficient to scare off the intruders. Next morning after my return I visited the site of all the excitement and found a nursery under some bushes where the mother had lain while the cub played around. Evidently this was the Median Tigress who

74

had returned to the area with her five-month-old cub. The curious phenomenon of the six trees being sprayed within a ninety-metre area was now explained: the Median Tigress had been marking the site of her intended nursery. Tara's reaction to her arrival was to shift her range to the south and east for, as I have already mentioned, tigresses with cubs will not usually tolerate other females.

At about this time an astonishing sequence of events took place, heralding the takeover of the range from its two residents – TM and Long Toes – by a male tiger. The usurper was in fact no stranger, and several years previously he himself had been the resident. I had named him Old Crooked Foot because of an injury to his right forepaw, which twisted outwards. Towards the end of 1977 he had suddenly vanished from the neighbourhood, but now it appeared he had come back to repossess his former range. As far as I am aware, the visits of Old Crooked Foot started when I saw his pugmarks near the Double Storey Machan one morning in mid-January, but it is possible that his approach may have begun earlier. Certainly Long Toes decided to move north at about this time. In disposing of TM, Old Crooked Foot's takeover bid was infinitely more deliberate and subtle, lasting from January until mid-April. What started as a probe up to the Double Storey Machan from the west was gradually combined with a series of calls which made the other tiger further aware of Old Crooked Foot's presence. Soon the probe was extended to the Planks and then the Croc Bend and beyond, with domination scrapes and rollings thrown in as an additional proof of his intention. Kills were still shared but chiefly on a proprietary basis by Old Crooked Foot. Gradually TM's visits became less frequent and the movement came full circle in mid-April when he abandoned his rights to the remnants of a highly-smelling kill near Chorleekh. Thereafter, apart from one further foray, he was no longer seen on the range that year. The whole episode bears witness to the tiger's remarkable lack of aggression in favourable conditions. Here were three of the most heavily armed solitary predators in the world and yet the exchange had taken place without violence or bloodshed.

With TM's departure Tara soon started associating with the

Median Tigress and her cub and also with the Big Tigress and her two cubs. The father the latter two was apparently Old Crooked Foot and by May 1979 they were about eight months old. Often the tigresses and their offspring would share their kills with Tara without friction; it seems that, provided the cubs are old enough, there is no reason why tigresses with young should not associate at kills.

With the rains not far off, I returned to the task of trying to get an identification photograph of Tara. The other tigers on the range, including Old Crooked Foot and the Median Tigress, all seemed to be amenable, but Tara with her more flighty ways still eluded me. This time I chose as my scene of operations a stretch of river about half a kilometre long between Tiger Haven and Leopard Haven which I named Tiger Reach. At this point in the river there is a lot of driftwood; conditioned by the action of water and sun and half-buried in the silt deposit of many years, the branches stick out of the water in grotesque twisted shapes. Among the debris of tangled roots which provides a certain amount of shelter, tigers will sit and cool themselves during the hot months of the year. Two spillways, bordered by luxuriant and dense ratwa grass, connect the river to the Mutana Tal, and the flood waters ebb and flow until finally, at the end of the rains, they drain into the Neora leaving the Mutana Lake full to the brim. Here the soil is always damp, and soft grasses make it an ideal resting place in the hottest weather. One spillway debouches into the river at the western end of the Reach, while the other runs past what I had selected as a baiting site and meets the river about 160 metres from the eastern end, where the gnarled roots of ancient trees lie half-submerged in topsy-turvey disorder. This was the spot I chose to set up a camera hide, about eighty metres from the central spillway, so that I could see along the entire stretch of the river to a third spillway to the east which came down to the escarpment.

The night after TM finally abandoned the range the Big Tigress, accompanied by her cubs, made a kill at the Tiger Reach site. A considerable portion was eaten and Jackson covered the remains with grass. However, when I arrived somewhat later in the morning, the grass had been partly uncovered and the tigress and her cubs had apparently moved off when they heard us approaching. I asked Jackson to put up a machan overlooking – but at some distance from – the kill because it was vital not to make a disturbance. From this vantage point I hoped to watch both the water and the kill-site. Unfortunately there was a large overhanging branch immediately in front of the kill which seemed too close to be tampered with, and mistakenly I allowed it to remain. Jackson sat on the machan and at about 10.30 a.m. he saw a large tigress approaching alone, but she moved off when she spotted a visitor who happened to be with us at the time. Later I climbed onto the machan and after a while saw a tigress moving along the spillway to the south towards the kill which she started to eat. I did not have binoculars with me, but only a 400mm lens attached to my camera, and the distance was about 160 metres in the splashy lighting of a jamun copse. Moreover, the errant branch which hung over the kill seemed even more prominent than before. Nevertheless, though no distinguishing marks were visible, this animal did look to me like Tara rather than the Big Tigress. I rested my camera on a cushion, attached it to the end of a walking stick, contorted myself to look under the construction which now took on the dimensions of a small tree, and took a series of highly unsatisfactory photographs. Shortly afterwards the tigress disappeared into the grass, but later she went to sit in the water at the head of the Reach. Unfortunately I had not yet built a hide on the other side of the river and was only able to watch her for a while before she moved back into cover. Once again Tara had evaded my camera.

Over the next few weeks Tiger Reach was a hive of tiger activity and I had several encounters which, from a photographic point of view, were rather frustrating. One day I sat behind the blind all morning but apart from a white stork, some paradise flycatchers and a few gaily coloured kingfishers, nothing came to the water. It was particularly hot and I wondered where Old Crooked Foot was cooling himself. I crossed the river, which was quite shallow at that point, and walked cautiously with my camera along a narrow pathway which had been cleared of leaves to another hide. As I passed the head of Tiger Reach there was an upheaval of water and the tiger, who had been hidden in the river behind a festoon of roots, saw me and disappeared up the opposite bank. I returned rather crestfallen but my cup of disappointment was by no means full. On my way back I suddenly saw the Big Tigress's two cubs scampering up the side of the central spillway; then, descending into the water, I caught a glimpse of the tigress behind an over-turned root. By this time I was so demoralized that I continued on my way through the water, ostrich-like, in the hope that the tigress might think herself invisible if I didn't look at her. However, by the time I surfaced at the other end the tigress had also disappeared and I carried on despondently home without having taken a single photograph.

On another occasion Jackson came in to report that the Big Tigress with her two cubs was sitting in the water at the spillway in front of the hide. By the time I got there they were moving along the bank, playing and climbing trees as they went. Eventually they crossed over to the north bank at a sandspit near the western end of the Reach and disappeared round the bend in the river. The cubs were growing up quickly, and from the multiple scratches I found on one of the baits it appeared that they were already assisting their mother at kills when they were only nine months old.

During this time Tara seemed to be avoiding Tiger Reach, though there were plenty of signs of her presence and indications that she was maturing into a fully-grown tigress. Her killing technique was being refined to deal with different classes of prey and recently she had come across a vigorous buffalo which she had felt unable to deal with in the proper fashion. She had therefore attacked it from the rear, and it was only after a prolonged struggle that she had succeeded in subduing the animal. On another occasion when killing a bait, she had seized it by the throat in the regulation manner, showing that she had learned her lessons well.

But once again the monsoon was threatening and with the first showers the tigers moved away. A few days later Tara came to cross the Junction Bridge near Tiger Haven for the second time that season. She wandered about indecisively near the Leopard

Bridge and sprayed a number of times before approaching; soon, however, independence reasserted itself, and though next night she killed a small bait and ate a little, she soon left to embark on her own pursuits.

I had to wait until early the following year before I finally succeeded in getting the photograph I needed. By then I realized that it had to be taken by night, and as my own equipment was not sophisticated enough for night pictures I sought the help of a young naturalist who possessed a motor-operated camera and a remote-control device. Tara was now regularly attending feeding sessions with Old Crooked Foot and the other tigers at the spillway site at Tiger Reach, and only fifty metres away there was a machan. We camouflaged the cameras and tried to muffle the sound of the motor, which was within a few metres of the kill, in the hope that the tigers would confuse the flash with some unseasonal summer lightning. This worked remarkably well, and in the photographs which emerged the left-cheek stripe matched the one in a picture taken of Tara when she was about fourteen months old. So too did the right eyespot. At last there could be no doubt in anybody's mind that Tara was alive. Her survival as a wild tigress had shown that it was indeed possible to take a zoo-born cub of the fifth generation and reintroduce her to her native habitat more than 8000 kilometres away.

During the monsoon that year Tara often hunted in the company of Old Crooked Foot in an area towards the south and east of Tiger Haven where they found stray cattle. But one day in the middle of October while the waters were still receding, Tara walked slowly along the opposite bank of the river in broad daylight. I called to her in an imitation *prusten* by which I had sought to enter her life while she was still with me, and she stood and watched me before spraying an overhanging branch. Once more she moved forward and I called to her vocally. She turned her head to look at me before moving on out of sight. An elderly lady who happened to visit Tiger Haven soon afterwards said that her grown-up daughter now behaved in the same way.

# Epilogue

The successful conclusion of any wildlife project is a source of great satisfaction, and when it demonstrates that a declining population can be restored to its original state, then the possibilities seem endless. Reactions are often debased by social stresses, but deep down in most humans is a concern for the underdog. Venerated in folklore and legend, the predator is everywhere under threat of extinction. Sport killing and the fur trade have taken their toll. Competition and the desire to eliminate a rival, and thereby acquire a status symbol, have served to drive the great predators to the point of no return, and when the legend is complete we will have to live with our regrets. For it has truly been said that we have not inherited the earth from our parents, but have borrowed it from our children.

Of the eight sub-species of tiger, four are either extinct or nearing extinction. Yet scientific quibbles still deny the integration of one sub-species with another, although they have both descended from a common ancestor in Siberia and adapted to their environment during the process of colonization. Minimal populations in restricted areas are all eventually doomed to genetic failure and extinction, and the only remedy is the translocation of animals by an international body in the belief that they will evolve a local morphology in the course of time. If the white rhino could be moved from South Africa, why can't we do the same with the tiger? Hitler's theory of *herrenvolk* was condemned, but are we being anthropomorphic when we apply the concept of 'One World' to save the tiger?

Wildlife is a truly international subject: the developed nations, who have largely destroyed their own wild animals, seek to preserve those of the developing countries. However, the government of the people by the people and for the people is strictly on a national basis, and in this lies the greatest danger to the preservation of wildlife. The fact that Tara came from Twycross Zoo in England and was integrated into an Indian National Park demonstrates that international co-operation is possible. Is it too much to hope that this might set an example for the future?

# Appendix

# The Future of the Tiger?

At the beginning of the twentieth century, the world tiger population was estimated at 100,000. In view of the alarming decline in numbers which has already occurred, has the dawning realization that the days of this animal are numbered at the hands of man come too late? I believe that the countdown has already started, and that this generation of tigers – with a possible remnant surviving into the next – will be the last. If for no other reason, the future existence of the super-predators is doubtful because they cannot compete with the greatest predator of all: man. Unless a slogan can be found which will appeal to the basic charity inherent in most human beings, we cannot mount the vital crusade necessary to salvage the lost cause of maintaining wildlife.

The concept of wild ungulate farms is now accepted as a source of cheap protein for the human race, but the scientists' argument that predators are the best wildlife managers in wilderness areas is nullified by man's arms technology and penchant for sport killing – albeit by culling the prime breeders and debasing the herds. A sad case in point is the United States which, by the scientific maintenance of 'sustained yields' for sport killing, has assumed the role hitherto played by the mountain lion and the wolf. The ungulates now exist on borrowed time, though they have gained some respite in that their status has been changed from that of vermin with a bounty on their heads to that of game animals which may be shot on possession of a permit. Conservation schemes are largely funded by these sport hunters, and it is a notable pointer to the strength of the hunter lobby that 97 per cent of Federal and State funding goes to the management of game animals. Other affluent countries have also depressed their predator populations in the interests of their hunter/farmer lobby.

The argument that wild animals act as guinea pigs in testing whether the environment is fit for human existence is in itself spurious, since surely the technology which gauges pollution and fits gas eliminators on motor cars can also test the environment? Until the basic premise that wildlife has a right to exist as a microcosm of natural evolution is accepted, no single entity will be safe. From a lowly creation a greater civilization may evolve, but once the principle of might over right is accepted, there is no argument to sustain, for example, the sanctimonious opposition to apartheid or white minority rule as a method of government.

Man is obviously the final arbiter so far as the continuing tenure of wildlife is concerned; but only when its protection has an emotional appeal for humanity will it cease to be treated as an intellectual problem presupposing a compromise solution – now seen by many as a euphemism for retreat. The slogan 'Save the Tiger' was of such emotional appeal that in record time 1.8 million dollars was collected, largely from schoolchildren. Yet *where* are we to save the tiger? Asia is overpopulated by a burgeoning human count, but would the United States, Great Britain or the Republic of Germany accept this devastating predator? A scientific edict frowns on the import of exotic faunal species, yet in the States the chukor is a game bird, Texas has more blackbuck than the whole of India and the chital has colonized Hawaii. The Third World has a monopoly of the spectacular predators, yet also a preponderance of humans living below the breadline. The National Parks in India are now probably too small and highly pressurized to sustain in perpetuity a viable genetic population of a predator so demanding as the tiger. Even in the Glacier National Park where there is supposed to be full environmental protection, two grizzlies — including one with cubs — were destroyed because they inflicted casualties on humans who were camping at forbidden sites against Park regulations. If a motorist is not hanged for running over a pedestrian who crosses the road against the light signal, what hope is there for an animal whose habitat is nowhere safe from intrusion? For the tiger with no concept of right or wrong, his world was made for *him*.

Instead of the impersonal call for complete environmental protection we now have a cry to save the world's master predator and his ecosystem. Yet do we have the crusaders? Democracy being government of, for and by the people, wildlife has no place in the official credo and exists at best on sufferance and usually as an expendable item in an exploding population. The politicians may consider *me* because I have a vote, but not my dog who has none. Wildlife fared best under authoritarian regimes, not because the ruler loved animals but because he wanted more to kill. Until there is some form of conservation vote so that wildlife can be represented in the parliaments of government, processes of attrition will continue despite the best of intentions. Finally there will be no room for wild animals, since they do not have the fundamental right to exist.

'Project Tiger' was spearheaded by a trustee of the World Wildlife Fund, which considered that of the eight subspecies at one time in existence, some were extinct, and some so threatened as to make their continued survival doubtful, India seemed to offer the best possibility of saving the tiger in terms of numbers and stability of government. A WWF contribution of a million dollars towards the implementation of the Project was accepted by the Prime Minister of India, and a Task Force was appointed to select areas and work on the logistics of the most comprehensive international conservation scheme hitherto undertaken. All seemed set fair for the 'New Look' of conservation as an international concern.

Soon, however, parochialism took over. The newly-appointed Chairman went on record as saying that the Project was primarily national in view of the country's major financial contribution.

The representative of WWF-International attended the first Task Force meeting and received such a chilly reception that he did not come again. The original euphoria soon evaporated and the Indian budget was pruned from 46 to 35 million rupees. Moreover, the various states were unwillingly committed to bearing half the expenditure of their individual projects without prior consultation. The Task Force submitted to the WWF an indent for a helicopter, four aircraft and other expensive items, but fortunately this was cancelled by the Prime Minister following representations made to her. These, however, were merely teething problems.

A census revealed the existence of 1,827 tigers, of whom 258 dwelt in the nine Project areas selected. Thus only 14 per cent of our tigers – some already in well protected areas – were initially chosen for the additional protection offered by the Project. While the future was not spelled out the primacy of commerial forestry operations was confirmed by a Task Force statement that though there would be a moratorium on these operations for a period of six years while the Project lasted, this loss would hopefully be recompensed by the additional maturity of the harvested timber at its close. This proviso, inserted at the instance of the Forest Department which by lack of executive forethought had become the custodians of wildlife, still looms threateningly over these forest areas.

In February 1979 an International Symposium on the Tiger was held in New Delhi, but since international delegates were few, an overall picture of the status of the tiger failed to come into focus. It did, however, provide a meeting place for those concerned, and lessons emerged which hopefully might be used for the forthcoming six-year plan period, though it was unfortunate that implementation was delayed due to a change in government. As was perhaps natural, the Symposium was dominated by the foresters, who by default have found themselves responsible for wildlife. As many as six papers contributed by a single entity were included in the agenda, with the result that a meaningful evaluation was not possible in the limited time available. What was manifest, however, was the foresters' desire to project an image of expertise despite lack of scientific background in wildlife management principles. This probably arose naturally from the wish to exclude foreign scientific expertise, which would in turn have opened a window for international concern over a project now promising to become a vested interest of the Forest Department. The loss of the Smithsonian Tiger Ecology Project because of this pressure aimed at excluding foreigners has set us back considerably, for we have failed to benefit from the modern methods of tranquillization and translocation as a means of solving population problems.

Paul Leyhausen, Chairman of the IUCN Cat Specialist Group, as member of the mid-term appraisal Committee for Project Tiger had suggested a possible 2 per cent increase in the tiger population. This cautious estimate was laughed to scorn by the modern forester planners as being too slow, and a laboratory estimate of 8 per cent was suggested. Considering that the classic work of Schaller on the Serengeti lion, conducted in a core area of approximately 3,800 sq. km. over a three-and-a-half-year period, postulated merely a 5.5 per cent increase in a predator with the social security of pride protection, an 8 per cent increase for the solitary tiger is out of the question. Even these figures of population dynamics are dwarfed by the stated overall increase of almost 25 per cent per annum in Project areas. Some areas have even registered an increase of 50 per cent but even allowing for expansions in area these claims need to be closely scrutinized. Corbett Park, which has lost 85 sq. km. of the best tiger habitat to the Ramgange Dam, has still registered an increase of nearly 14 per cent.

The tiger population of the country as a whole has registered an increase of 6 per cent, or more than the lion of the Serengeti National Park which has been known to maintain a density of as much as 3-5 sq. km. Considering the pressures which wildlife outside Project areas still suffer, these figures are absurd, and merely indicate faulty and wishful census methods. A vivid example is the census conducted in the Dudhwa National Park in 1979. No officer was present during this operation despite its importance, and the pugmark tracings were taken by untrained wildlife guards and forest guards. From 240 tracings submitted to the Deputy Director of the Park, it seemed that some of the tigers had five toes! From then on it was simplicity to produce an *ad hoc* total figure of fifty-one. The next census will perforce have to register another increase since bureaucracy thrives on such statistics. Other census figures could be equally unreliable.

The tiger, instead of being a symbol for complete environmental protection, is becoming a status symbol for the foresters who man the key posts in Project areas. An aura of secrecy surrounds the inner working of these *sanctum sanctorums,* where naturalists, tourists and conservationalists are not allowed and non-officials are regarded with hostility. Euphoric reports periodically reverberate in the cement jungles of the capital, however muted the call of the tiger in his habitat.

The most unfortunate development in our constitution was the allocation of responsibility for wildlife, initially a bureaucratic convenience that as wildlife lived in forest areas they should be under the aegis of the Forest Department. For a trained forester, forestry operations will be always paramount, especially when compared with other responsibilities without earning capacity. A tree felled means loss of habitat for birds and small mammals. Moreover, being constitutionally a State subject, there is always pressure by the local politician who depends for his vote on the villager whose cattle are killed by the tiger and whose crops are grazed by the deer. It is unfortunately true that wildlife can now only exist by virtue of the goodwill of the human inhabitants living in peripheral areas; this could be possible if the government assisted them to build permanent houses and thus relieved pressure on the forests, but instead there is increasing infiltration into park areas to seek materials for temporary hutments. If these villagers benefited from the presence of a wildlife area, they would wish the Park well.

By some centripetal convolution of administration most political and bureaucratic talent appears to gravitate to Central Government, where objectivity of outlook and breadth of vision seem to end. The States are mainly left with local obscurants and party bosses whose administrative horizon is bounded by the confines of their village or the next election. Such individuals would fell all the forests and give the land cleared to the landless, kill all wildlife and feed the hungry, by which time their term of office would be over and their successors would reap the whirlwind. Unfortunately this is our administrative set-up at present, and a compromise solution is sought for every wildlife problem. There are 2,000 tigers in 4 per cent of habitat. There are 650 million humans. How long can we compromise?

Prospects of the Tara story ever being repeated seem remote, in spite of the fact that a rehabilitation experiment could be tried again with every hope of success under proper conditions. The Second World Conference on the Breeding of Endangered Species in Captivity was held in London in 1976, and a similar conference had taken place in Texas in 1973. Their mandate was the replenishing of wild stocks when necessary. Owing to lack of a meaningful rapport with countries where such endangered species do exist, we have a confused situation – induced over-breeding among the great cats due to increased potential under captive conditions; limited commercial interchange with other zoos; followed by contraceptive pills for tigresses and vasectomies for unwanted lions as the bottom drops out of the market. The newly-formed CITES (Convention for the International Control of Trade in Endangered Species) should deal with this, but the unfavourable reaction of individual countries is almost certain. I conclude that governments of the countries in which these animals are found will not make the attempt because basically, whatever the international climate, the human does not want a rival predator. From the days when he cowered in his cave while more powerful carnivores prowled outside, through medieval times when – armed with a flintlock – he barely held his own, to the modern era when equipped with the ultimate in weapon technology he gunned them down from the safety of tall trees in the name of 'sport', this attitude persists in spite of the lip service paid to conservation schemes. When the last tiger has gone to its forebears, only a few crocodile tears will be shed for a vanished legend.

In my district, government figures show that thirty-two

humans have been killed by tigers, but a few of these casualties might be ascribed to intraspecific feuds in which the tiger becomes the scapegoat! Most of these man-eating cases arise from the fact that, because of destruction and degradation of cover in the forests, breeding tigresses have moved into the temporarily attractive cover of sugar-cane fields. As harvesting progresses the habitat shrinks, wild prey species become decimated by crop-protection firearms (issued as a form of political patronage) and the tigress – handicapped by famished and immobile cubs and accustomed to constant human presence – is on a collision course. Since last year three tigresses have been declared man-eaters, and two tigers and three tigresses have been shot. In no instance have the cubs been successfully rescued. Thus we treat our national animal. The remedy surely is to tranquillize these hard-pressed animals and translocate them to favourable areas, but it is easier to kill them and apportion their skins to the murderers – even in death wildlife must pay for itself. So long as foreign expertise is successfully excluded in order that our small-time bureaucracy may gain kudos, the war of attrition will continue to its logical conclusion.

An alarming indication is the attitude of the Forest Department as influenced their political masters, as evidenced when a sub-committee of Field Directors from Project Tiger was nominated by the Indian government to study the incidence of man-eating in the Kheri district. The leader of the team, described in typically extravagant prose by UNI as 'The topmost living authority on tigers in the world', has in a verbose and highly conjectural report gone on record as saying that his mandate was to remove the most sensitive socio-ecological conflict between the local man and the man-eater. Later on, however, it becomes clear that his solution to this conflict is the removal of the tiger. While admitting that the habitat has become so degraded and restricted, and the natural prey species so decimated, that a drastic environmental and ecological change has taken place in living conditions, the report makes the ignorant and confused statement that due to restricted habitat conditions and exposure to the proximity of the tiger, reproductive dynamics were increasing contrary to

Malthusian principles *(sic)*. Emphasizing that overbreeding by these famished tigers has included a spillover of resident populations, the report recommends destruction (by shooting or poisoning) of what they term aberrant and indisciplined tigers, and their ultimate utilization as a commercial resource. Regarding the killing of two innocent tigers, they casually excuse this as being due to enthusiasm for killing the man-eater as soon as possible!

The report pontificates that captive breeding and rehabilitation is not possible, despite my claim to have restored a tiger and leopards to their natural habitat. It asserts 'My five-year-old foster daughter Khairi [a tigress] may continue to move freely in open forest during brief periods under watchful studies. She is not intended to be rehabilitated in nature.' Perhaps the fact that Tara the zoo-born returned to her natural home, does not appeal to the forester who has inflicted the final indignity of bondage on a free-born tigress. But is the tiger safe with such people in charge?

The greatest danger arising from exploding population and shrinking habitat is that human intrusion will increase, unless we can rationalize wildlife habitats into viable ecosystems to the exclusion of all biotic pressures.

Over the ages the tiger displayed phenomenal adaptability. From the frozen caves of Siberia he has colonized the steamy rain forests of Sumatra and Java under pressure from expanding populations. He has crossed high mountain passes to extend his sway to the shores of the Caspian Sea. He has evaded the proximity of humans while the great submontane forests of Nepal existed as the ultimate and selective tiger breeding grounds. He has avoided humans not because of innate inferiority but because all animals shun the unfamiliar. Man is *in* the jungle but not *of* the jungle; he walks by day, wears clothes, talks loudly and indulges in uncouth gestures. The tiger, secretive hunter in the long shadows of the moon, walks alone. But now the last bastion appears likely to fall when, deprived of prey animals, famished predators prowling a degraded habitat during daylight hours come to terms with their oppressors. The tiger has become a part of the folklore and legend of the lands which he has colonized. Because of his secretive ways, mystic power and desire to keep away from the human invader, fantasy has taken over from knowledge which was in any case based merely on the unnatural reactions of hunted and harassed animals. From his formidable capacity to harm and injure has grown a conviction of his supernatural association with the powers of darkness and evil. From his savagery when wounded and pursued has emerged an image of diabolical ferocity. However, medieval times also lent him a reverence and awe which allowed him a sacrificial levy and even sought to excuse his depredations by a compulsive elemental association with human evil.

Now with his back to the wall, as the tiger fights to survive he needs the understanding and sympathy of civilized humanity. He has lost ground which he can never regain. All he needs is a small portion of habitat where he can maintain a genetic viability, and a favourable ecosystem of habitat and prey animals – free from biotic interferences, for wherever man goes he creates inbalances which he shortsightedly terms progress. This is surely not too much to ask when it is remembered that this fraction of habitat, even if released to human endeavour, will merely sustain our democratic 'survival of the sickest' for a fraction of a second in the aeons of evolution.

The emergence of the man-eater in its present setting is the first sign of growing human population pressurizing an ecosystem, for with less spectacular animals the reaction is not so dramatic. Man-eaters have been written about extensively by Corbett and Anderson, but it must be realized that these books have a commercial bias similar to that of a detective story writer. The gruesome killings, the subtle deductions, the narrow escapes and breathless denouement when right triumphs over wrong, the steady aim of the intrepid shikari is matched by the quickness on the draw of the master detective, is all a part of the build-up. Can anyone deny poetic licence to the shikari – so essential a requirement for the fiction writer? In the desire to write sensational true stories both Corbett and Anderson, perhaps unintentionally, did the tiger a disservice by not examining in detail why he or the leopard become man-eaters. I say 'unintentionally' because I knew Jim Corbett well; while he was our first conservationist, he was also in the midst of avid hunters to whom he was an idealist born out of his generation.

Corbett listed the causes of man-eating as old age, wounds and the habit being genetically passed to the offspring. Anderson, in his desire to produce dramatic potboilers, does not find it worthwhile to examine the causes, though both he and his son bewail the destruction by poachers of wild animals, after each killing. Old age can be ruled out straight away – if this was so, there would always be a few man-eaters eking out their closing years on a diet of human flesh. Wounds do not generally cause this aberration, although a tigress I subsequently shot took to man-eating after her jaw and canines had been broken by a poacher's gun. One gut-shot tiger lived a month in Bellrasin in North Kheri; a tiger caught in a trap and speared in the rump died five weeks later of septicaemia in the midst of habitation near a pond. A sub-adult with a porcupine quill through his lung died of starvation in the centre of human habitation. Two male tigers, each with a broken forepaw, lived near cultivated areas for two years; they were then shot, one by a tourist company, as potential man-eaters. Heredity plays no part either, except that cubs may share their mother's human meal.

The basis of every man-eating condition is prey scarcity. In the case of the majority of Jim Corbett's man-eating tigers this habit was triggered by injury from porcupine quills. However, porcupines are not generally considered to be a delicacy for the great cats, and though as hand-reared animals Prince and Tara both killed porcupines, not only were they very careful not to get injured while doing so but displayed no great desire to eat them. Tara as a wild tigress killed and ate an infant porcupine and chased an adult, but abandoned pursuit when she found she only got a mouthful of quills. An old acquaintance of mine, the black tiger, chased a porcupine over an acre of land, occasionally spitting out a mouthful of quills, before being able to seize it by the back of the head. However, after this 'academic killing' he did not bother to eat it. Corbett's man-eaters who got their mouths and paws full of quills were starving, and seized the rodent with impulsive avidity

95

instead of the normal precision with which a tiger launches his attack. Thereafter the prevailing condition of prey scarcity was aggravated by the agony of suppurating sores which brought them in contact with man; even then they did not live exclusively on a human diet but presumably scavenged when able to do so.

Under normal conditions man is not a prey species because he is not identified by the tiger as belonging to his forest. Tara's Male was killing baits regularly, but one night I placed a piece of sacking on the buffalo to protect it from frost. The tiger sat and watched it for a long time before moving away, and only killed the next night after the sack had been removed. Long Toes did the same when a small thatch roof was protecting the bait, and Old Crooked Foot sat and watched a bait from 8 p.m. onwards because a 12-V light had been placed above it — only killing after the battery discharged. Many myths have been propagated about the great cats' taste for blood, including the classic example of the pet lion who was licking his master's hand as he slept; soon the rasping tongue drew blood, and the lion ate the master. I kept leopards and a tiger over a period of eight years, and although their large sharp claws inadvertently drew blood as they played with me they merely licked it up and that was all. Compulsion combined with mercurial temperaments enables them to go for long stretches without a meal, and I would plead most emphatically that stories of their excesses should be dispassionately investigated before they are condemned for crimes which even in the case of humans can arise from necessity. When air passengers marooned in the Andes ate each other's dead bodies from necessity, survivors were not considered criminals or cannibals, and indeed a best-selling novel was written about them. The cane-fields harbouring a tiger who becomes a man-eater by necessity are grim places for the poor crop owner, where terror stalks the life he risks to feed and clothe his family. But within the fields are cubs whose mother — deprived of habitat — has littered in an agricultural crop, and who starve because her milk has dried as prey animals have been slaughtered by poacher and crop-protection guns. Both need a measure of sympathy which only one receives.

Soon we will lose our tigers as our increasing population

impinges on diminishing habitats. It is essential that wildlife habitats should be inviolate, and that, before it is too late, tigers who have been displaced should be immobilized and translocated to other suitable areas. Since these compulsively famished animals are usually tigresses with cubs, they are unlikely to suffer intraspecific aggression because single tigresses are not territorial. Male tigers may encounter territorial aggression, but conservationists will admit it is preferable for one tiger to naturally eliminate another rather than that the entire species should be pilloried because of a stigma for which they are not ultimately responsible.

While Tara was being hand-reared by me she was treated as a Park attraction, and photographers and press correspondents came to see her. After she returned to the wild the authorities rejected the experiment as one of which they were unaware and for which they had not given permission, though they knew it had received clearance from the highest authority and that they would never have given their consent once that government fell. They are adamant in refusing to accept the possibility of such an introduction to the wild and claim that a tigress brought up by humans will always remain imprinted. In support of this argument they quote the example of Khairi, a tigress in Orissa (mentioned on p.93) whose dignity has been bartered by her upbringing in human surroundings and who is now perforce denied her natural functions of association with a male tiger. They claim, perhaps hopefully, that Tara is now probably dead from poisoning, has been killed by another tiger, or even destroyed as one of the man-eaters which they reluctantly *(sic)* have had to slaughter.

Tigers have no passports and need no visas. Indian tigers are found in Nepal, Indo-Chinese tigers in Kampuchea and Siberians in China. When Americans say, 'Save the Tiger' they must be prepared to compensate the cultivator whose bullock he has killed. Wildlife should be an international concern, yet national governments of the people are motivated by fear that co-operation on an international scale will threaten the very freedom which they refuse to grant animals as a natural right.

TARA – A TIGRESS

Inveterate pessimist though I am, I still hope against hope that the tiger will see its way into the twenty-first century.

# Bibliography

Aspinall, J., *The Best of Friends* (London, 1976).

Brander, A. Dunbar, *Wild Animals in Central India* (London, 1923).

Champion, F. W., *With a Camera in Tiger-land* (London, 1927).

Corbett, Jim, *Man-eaters of Kumaon* (London, 1957).

Mountfort, Guy, *Tigers* (London, 1973).

Sankhala, K. S., *Tiger* (London, 1978).

Schaller, G. B., *The Deer and the Tiger* (Chicago, 1967).

Schaller, G. B., *The Serengeti Lion* (Chicago, 1972).

Singh, Arjan, *Tiger Haven* (London, 1973).

Stracey, P. D., *Tigers* (London, 1968).

The work of conservation and rehabilitation is carried on at Tiger Haven entirely through voluntary contributions. Tiger Haven is not government sponsored and depends on the goodwill and generosity of those concerned for the future of endangered species.

For further information please write to:

The International Trust for Nature Conservation
Wood Nash and Winters,
6 Raymond Buildings,
Gray's Inn,
LONDON W.C.2.